SECRET OF DEATH VALLEY

**Center Point
Large Print**

**This Large Print Book carries the
Seal of Approval of N.A.V.H.**

SECRET OF DEATH VALLEY

William Heuman

Center Point Publishing
Thorndike, Maine

This Center Point Large Print edition
is published in the year 2005 by arrangement with
Golden West Literary Agency.

Copyright © 1952 by William Heuman.
Copyright © renewed 1980 by the Estate of William Heuman.

All rights reserved.

The text of this Large Print edition is unabridged. In other
aspects, this book may vary from the original edition. Printed in
Thailand. Set in 16-point Times New Roman type.

ISBN 1-58547-547-5

Library of Congress Cataloging-in-Publication Data

Heuman, William.
    Secret of Death Valley / William Heuman.--Center Point large print ed.
    p. cm.
    ISBN 1-58547-547-5 (lib. bdg. : alk. paper)
    1. Death Valley (Calif. and Nev.)--Fiction. 2. Large type books. I. Title.

PS3558.E7997S43 2005
813'.54--dc22

                                                                2004017859

Chapter One

For two solid hours Hamp Cameron had lain on the sagging hotel bed, watching a sunbeam moving across the grimy, cracked plaster wall, feeling the heat like a blanket pressing down upon him. At four in the afternoon he got up, walked to the dresser, and poured himself another glass of water, emptying the big white pitcher. The water was warm from standing in the hot room all day, and it did not slake his thirst.

He remembered hearing a man discuss that fact on the train down here to Mormon on the edge of Death Valley. You could drink all day, and at the end of it still be thirsty. The heat pulled the moisture out of your body, evaporating it, and you needed more, always more.

Putting the empty glass down, he returned to the bed and sat down on the edge of it, his hundred and ninety pounds making the weak springs groan. He felt himself listening for sounds—sounds in the daytime and sounds in the night—the way he'd been listening now for twenty-two long months since he'd taken up the trail.

He heard someone moving around in the room adjoining his, and the strange, almost ludicrous thought came to him that perhaps his man was in there, separated from him by a few inches of plaster and lath through which a bullet could go like a knife through cheese.

He sat there, listening, his head pounding, breathing faster, the way he always did when he fancied his quarry was close by. His gray eyes receded a little in his head,

5

and then he reached for the gun holster that hung from the bedpost, sliding the Smith and Wesson .44 from the leather. He broke it to examine the cylinder, and then he put the gun back.

Rubbing his big hands together, he stared at the faded shade and the tawdry curtains across the window, the hot glare of the Southern California sun whitening the edges of the shade. He thought of other hotel rooms in which he had sat and waited on afternoons like this, waited for the night and the long chance that he would spot his man in the crowd around a faro table, or at a bar, or coming down a boardwalk toward him. Always he had been too late, a day, two days, a few hours.

Off in the distance he heard a train whistle, the train that had brought him here at noon this day, now headed back toward San Francisco. It was a lonely sound, like a train whistle in the night, only this was broad daylight in a strange and silent town. He had never been in a town before where men remained indoors during the noon hours. At high noon today he had walked down a silent, almost deserted street to the hotel, and yet as he passed the rows of sun-dried, unpainted, false-front houses and saloons he'd had the queer feeling that all hell was about to break loose, and that this was the calm before the storm.

He was unable to account for this feeling except for the fact that for nearly two years he had lived alone and for a purpose. He had lived with every sense alerted, listening for sounds that did not come, watching for that which never appeared.

Mormon, on the edge of Death Valley, was the railhead for the new borax industry. There had been much talk in Frisco concerning this flaky, cotton-ball substance that twenty-mule teams were snaking out of the pit of hell. It was a new industry, and a tremendously profitable one, he'd heard, with several outfits in Mormon competing with each other.

Hamp listened to the train whistle dying away in the distance, and then he heard another sound from the opposite direction, from the direction of Death Valley itself, a rumbling sound as of heavy wheels, and the rattle of chains and harness.

Walking to the window, he raised the shade slightly and looked out past the curtain. Directly opposite this Paradise Hotel at which he was staying was the office of Imperial Borax, the lower floor of a large two-story structure. He had noticed the name in gilt letters on the plate-glass window as he came down the street that noon.

Looking across the wide, dusty street now, he saw the door open and a man come out, a blocky, broad-shouldered, blunt-nosed man with a stub of cigar in his mouth. He walked with a peculiar rolling motion as he came out to the edge of the boardwalk and stood there, staring up the street toward the wagons.

Hamp watched him flip the cigar butt out into the road, and from this little action immediately formed a vague dislike for the man, even though he knew that it was foolish. There was a certain arrogance about the man—the way he tossed the cigar butt away, and the manner in which he stood there on the edge of the walk, flat-footed, solid legs spread a little, one hand hooked in his vest pocket.

Other people were coming out on the street now, from houses, from saloons, having heard the wagons, and Hamp sensed the fact that a borax outfit was rolling into Mormon, and because the industry was still new, this was a matter of interest to the public.

He had his look at the people in the street, experiencing only a mild disappointment when he did not spot his man. He did not expect Rob Jensen to be moving about in broad daylight. Jensen was a gambling man, and gambling men, like owls, saw little of the daylight. If he were in Mormon he wouldn't be in circulation till after dusk, when the saloons and gambling houses came alive.

As Hamp watched, the long string of mules came into view, ten teams of them, twenty animals hooked to the long chain. He'd seen a half-dozen teams hooked to the big ore wagons up in the Virginia City mine fields, but never ten teams.

When the borax wagons came into sight he realized why they needed that much mule power. The wagons were enormous, two of them hooked together, with a water tank rolling along in the rear. They were by far the biggest vehicles Hamp had ever seen, and he studied them with interest.

A driver rode the lead wagon with a swamper handling the brake on the tandem. The wagon beds were at least sixteen feet long, six feet deep, and four feet wide. The huge hind wheels were taller than a man, with tires at least eight inches wide and an inch thick. The hubs of the wheels were a foot and a half in diameter.

Both wagons were loaded to the tops with sacks of borax, a tremendous load from the way the big wheels dug into the dust of the road. The outfit rolled to a stop in front of the Imperial Borax office, both driver and swamper working the brakes, and the driver whooping at the mules.

The blocky, flat-nosed man who had come out of the office spoke for a few moments with the driver, who remained up on the seat. Through the closed window, closed to keep out the heat, Hamp could hear his voice, heavy, demanding, a man who wanted his answers immediately and without reservations.

After a while the outfit rolled on again, heading for the railroad siding. Hamp watched the small crowd disappear into the buildings again, and then he lowered the shade.

At five o'clock he went downstairs for another pitcher of water and washed his face and hands, feeling a little better, even though the room was as hot as ever. In heat like this he didn't think it cooled off till well past midnight, if it cooled at all.

With the Smith and Wesson strapped around his waist, his black coat covering it, he went down to the desk. The clerk told him there was an eating place next door to the hotel. As he scanned the register, the clerk, a thin, bony man with spectacles, watched him curiously.

"Looking for someone, mister?" he asked.

"Thin man," Hamp told him. "Light blond hair, narrow face."

Green eyes, he thought, like pieces of jade. Eyes a woman could fall for, with long lashes.

The clerk shook his head. "Town's full of strangers these days," he said. "That one I don't know."

Hamp asked no more questions. The bartender in Frisco had said he'd thought Jensen had gone down to Mormon, but he wasn't sure, and there was a good possibility that this was another false lead, another cold trail.

The heat hit him when he stepped out into the street. It seemed to come up from the ground, to move toward him in waves, one hotter than the next. Through it men moved sluggishly, all the energy drained out of them, and he wondered how they could keep those big wagons rolling down there in the Valley, where he was told it often rose to 130 in the shade, and never any shade.

In the lunchroom he had a meal of ham and eggs with a large portion of baked beans. He was hungry now, but he didn't stuff himself, knowing that much food would make him sluggish, and tonight there was the possibility that he would require speed of hand.

Finishing the meal, he touched a match to a cigar and sat back in the chair. He'd taken a corner table, facing the door, and as each diner came in, he scanned the man closely, realizing that it was very possible that his man had already disguised himself—with a mustache, or by dyeing his hair.

A tall, raw-boned, sandy-haired man with a star on his vest came in to eat as Hamp was lighting his cigar. He was a homely man with a gaunt face, wide mouth, and prominent nose, but his eyes were good, brown, clean.

The law in Mormon looked at Hamp in the corner,

recognized him as another stranger, and then promptly dismissed him. Hamp heard the counter man call him Bill.

A young Chinese boy was waiting on the tables, and as he started to pick up the dishes, Hamp said to him casually, "Friend of mine eats here sometimes. Thin man with blond hair and a narrow face. His hair is silky. Seen him around lately?"

The boy shook his head, and Hamp frowned, the first real doubt coming to his mind that he had made a mistake riding all the way down here to Mormon. He should have made more inquiries in San Francisco instead of accepting the bartender's statement that his man had gone on to Mormon.

It was nearly seven o'clock in the evening now, and still quite early to start his search, but he was restless, and he had waited all day for this. Paying his bill at the counter, he stepped outside on the walk, the half-smoked cigar in his mouth, and he stood on the edge of the walk, not quite sure which direction to take.

He heard the screen door open and close behind him, and when he turned his head slightly he caught a glimpse of shining metal on a man's vest. The law of Mormon came out to the edge of the walk and paused there, staring across the street at a saloon.

When Hamp glanced at him he turned his head, smiled faintly, and said, "Hell of a hot town."

Hamp nodded, but he didn't say anything. The law man went on casually, "Strangers comin' here don't stay more than two days. It gets them. You stay for a week, an' it's not too bad. Water starts to dry up in your body."

"That right?" Hamp murmured.

"Name's Buckley," the Sheriff said. "Bill Buckley."

Hamp looked at him then, understanding that the man wanted to be friendly. He held out his hand and said, after a moment's hesitation, "Cameron."

They shook hands and Bill Buckley put a cigar in his mouth. He said as he was lighting it, his hands cupped, speaking around the cigar, "You after borax, too?"

Hamp shrugged. "Just looking," he said.

"Big business in this town," Bill Buckley told him. "Big profits. Valley and Imperial outfits can haul the stuff to the railroad for one cent a pound and sell it by the carload at ten cents. That's profit."

Hamp nodded. He'd been in other boom towns—gold towns, silver towns, copper towns in Montana. This was borax, the stuff from which they made drugs, he'd been told, and another boom. It was all the same and it did not interest him.

To be polite he said, "Reckon it takes a man to get the stuff out of the Valley, though."

Bill Buckley laughed softly. "You believe it or not," he chuckled, "but a woman's doin' the major part of it now. It is a man's job, though." When Hamp looked at him curiously, Buckley went on, "Borax Charlie Graham was the first man in Death Valley. He set up the system, the big wagons, the twenty-mule teams. He was a man for system, and his wagons rolled on time, rain or shine, as they say, although there's not much rain in the Valley."

"I saw the rigs," Hamp stated. "Reckon they're built for rugged travel."

"Charlie died a year ago," Sheriff Buckley said. "His daughter, Sheila, runs the outfit."

Hamp nodded, but he was losing interest now, anxious to be gone. The old fever was on him again and he was restless. Men were coming out of doorways, passing on the boardwalk, turning into the saloons and gambling houses. Very slowly, the way a cat emerges from sleep, the town of Mormon came alive. The odor of frying food assailed his nostrils. To the right, a short distance down the street, a piano was tinkling in a saloon.

"Have a drink with me before you leave, Cameron," Sheriff Buckley invited.

"Obliged," Hamp said, and then the strange thought came to him that perhaps he wouldn't be leaving. The man with the corn-silk hair might be leaving, and he, Hamp Cameron, might be dead!

Chapter Two

Leaving Buckley, Hamp turned north along the main street, walking slowly, his hat pulled low over his eyes, glancing into each saloon as he passed. The bars were beginning to fill up, but he didn't see the man he was looking for.

He walked past nine saloons on one side of the street, and as he was coming up again toward the railroad station he came abreast of a lighted office window. In large gold letters on the window were the words "Valley Borax Company."

Slowing down a little, out of idle curiosity, Hamp

13

glanced inside. The office was still open, lamps burning. A girl with dark chestnut hair stood in front of a desk, her back toward Hamp. She was talking with a tall man in a brown suit who was facing the window, standing on the other side of the desk, and when Hamp looked at him, his heart started to pump wildly. The blood rushed to his face, and he took one quick step backward out of the light of the window.

The man in the brown suit had corn-silk hair, wavy, parted in the middle, exactly like Jensen. Hamp Cameron recovered himself. He was breathing hard, the sweat standing out on his face as he realized his mistake. The man behind the desk had only the same peculiar light-blond hair, but after that the resemblance stopped.

He was a taller man, heavier in the shoulders. His face was full, with a square chin; Jensen had a narrow, pointed chin. This man was handsome, well built, poised, far removed from the despicable, slinking creature Hamp sought.

Still breathing heavily, Hamp continued on his way, but not before he'd had a side glimpse of the girl's face as she turned slightly. She was young, not more than twenty-one or -two. It was the kind of face a man did not often see in a boom town, where painted women abounded. Hamp had run across his share of the latter; he'd seen too little of the former.

She had a small, well-shaped nose and mouth, and when she smiled it was as if a light broke out on her face. Hamp would have liked to take a longer look at her, but other people were passing on the street, and he had to go on.

14

He moved on to the next saloon, and the next, until he reached the railroad station, and then he crossed the street leisurely and proceeded down the other side. He understood that this was just a preliminary survey. Very possibly his man was still not abroad; and if he were in town, he might not make his appearance until later in the evening, when the real gambling began.

Several times as he walked Hamp reached inside his coat to feel the cold butt of the Smith and Wesson. It was a short-barreled gun, blunt and deadly.

Passing the Valley Borax office on the opposite side of the street this time, Hamp looked across the wide road. He saw the man in the brown suit just coming out of the door, angling across the street in his direction, and as both men continued to walk, the blond-haired man came up on Hamp's side within a half-dozen feet of him. He glanced at Hamp idly and moved on ahead of him, turning into the Death Valley Saloon.

Hamp watched him pause at the bar and chat with Sheriff Bill Buckley. There were only a few other drinkers at the bar as yet, and Hamp continued on his way.

He was dry now, after eating, and he turned in at the next saloon, a smaller one named the Piute, which was almost directly opposite the hotel at which he was staying. He didn't bother this time to look in before pushing open the bat-wing doors.

He noticed idly that there were a half-dozen men at the bar, their backs toward him. A sweating, fat-faced bartender was pushing a glass of beer toward one customer, and he glanced at Hamp as he came in.

The man directly ahead of Hamp as he came through the door had a glass of liquor tilted to his mouth, and he was standing with one boot up on the bar rail. He was dressed in black, black coat, black hat.

As Hamp hesitated, not certain whether to go to the left or right end of the bar, the man in black set the glass down and turned around to start for the door.

Hamp took one step to the right and stopped as if he had run into a concrete wall. The man coming away from the bar was slim, thin-faced. He had a wedge of a chin, a narrow nose, a weak mouth, and a pasty complexion. His eyes were green jade, and his hair, under the black, flat-crowned hat, was pale blond, silky, like corn silk.

The slender man took one look at Hamp, and then backed toward the bar, eyes staring, mouth beginning to twitch. His pasty skin suddenly became blotched. He opened and closed his mouth, and then his slim, white right hand darted inside his coat.

He came out with a big Navy Colt that looked tremendous in that slender hand. A man at the bar who had seen the movement let out a quick, startled yelp, and then the Navy gun boomed.

Hamp Cameron fired a fraction of a second later, just as the bullet from the Colt nicked the sleeve of his coat on the left side. He started to walk forward after firing the first shot, which had knocked the slender man back against the bar as if he'd been hit with a heavy club.

Less than a dozen feet had separated them when they recognized each other. Hamp Cameron narrowed the distance to eight and then six feet, walking forward slowly, squeezing on the trigger, emptying one chamber and then another. He stopped shooting when his gun was almost touching the black coat of the slender man, and he stopped only because the six cylinders of the gun were empty, and even then he continued to click the hammer automatically.

The man with the corn-silk hair had been hit in the chest with the first bullet. The lead that had followed seemed to pin him back against the bar, preventing him from falling. He had fired one shot at Hamp, and after that his gun was useless.

Hamp watched him sag along the bar, stumble into one gulping, white-faced drinker six feet away, knock down a half-filled beer glass, and then pitch face forward to the sawdust-strewn floor. He lay on his face, his black hat fallen from his head, his long blond hair in the sawdust.

For several long moments after the echoes of the last shot Hamp had fired had died away, there was silence in the Piute Saloon. Outside, Hamp could hear people yelling excitedly.

In the saloon the man whose beer glass had been spilled was saying weakly, "This other feller pulled a gun first. I seen him. He pulled it out o' his coat an' started to shoot. I was watchin' him."

Hamp Cameron shoved the Smith and Wesson back into his waistband and turned and walked toward the door. He felt no emotion, no joy, no satisfaction, nothing. He was like a dead man, and his brain was not working.

He was aware of the fact that Sheriff Bill Buckley

brushed past him as he went out through the bat-wing doors, and a crowd was running toward the saloon now that the shooting had stopped. They crowded around the doors, looking inside, ignoring him as he went out to the edge of the walk and put one shoulder against the wooden upright supporting the overhead awning.

He stood there, staring down into the dust of the road. There were tremendous changes taking place inside him, and he had to wait to see what kind of man he had become. Vaguely he realized that he should have been feeling elated now, or if not elated, at least satisfied that he had accomplished what he had set out to do nearly two years before. His cause had been righteous. He had succeeded in his mission of vengeance, and he should have been satisfied, but he wasn't. He knew that very clearly. It was empty; it was nothing.

A man was calling from the door of the saloon, "Somebody git Doc Haskell."

Hamp Cameron watched a big, round, silvery moon swing up above the rim of the hotel roof. He had never seen a moon so large or so distinct as this one.

Across the road, also, the door of the Valley Borax office had opened and the girl Hamp had seen inside came out to look across at the saloon from which the shots had come. Hamp could see her face indistinctly in the dim light.

Men were still hurrying up from various saloons along the street, running past the spot where Hamp stood. He heard the step on the boards close by, and when he turned his head he saw Sheriff Bill Buckley coming up.

Buckley said thoughtfully, "So you found what you came for, Cameron."

Hamp nodded. He said nothing.

"You knew the man?" Buckley asked.

"I knew him," Hamp said briefly.

Buckley stood there with his hands in his hip pockets, staring down into the dust of the road. "Plenty o' witnesses," he said, "to prove that this chap shot first. We don't have anything against you, Cameron. Plain self-defense."

Hamp shrugged his shoulders slightly.

"He's not dead yet," Buckley went on, "an' he wants to see you. He won't last more than a few minutes."

Hamp looked at the man. The request had caught him completely by surprise, and he wasn't sure what he should do.

"Doc Haskell's up to Willow Springs," Sheriff Buckley said. "Nothin' we kin do for this *hombre*. Reckon you put enough lead in him to kill three men."

Hamp grimaced. He pushed away from the post on an impulse and walked toward the saloon, shouldering his way through the crowd around the entrance. Bill Buckley came behind him, and as they were going past through the doors the Sheriff said, "He's in the back room to the right."

Hamp saw the cluster of men around the open doorway to the right of the bar. They let him through when he approached, several of them staring at him curiously.

A bartender was inside, bending over the dying man on the couch. The blond-haired man lay with his face to the wall, and Hamp could see his features already beginning to settle into the rigidity of death. He stood at the foot of the couch, trying to remember that he hated this man, even though he was dying.

"Goes by the name of Torgeson in this town," Bill Buckley said. "Been around Mormon a month or so. Took him for a gamblin' man."

The man on the couch turned his head. His eyes were a dull green now, and he stared at Hamp for several moments before saying anything. When he spoke his voice was surprisingly clear. He said, "Figured you'd stopped looking for me, Cameron."

Hamp shook his head. He saw Buckley walk to the door and close it after sending the bartender out. The Sheriff of Mormon stood with his back to the door, arms folded.

"How is she?" the man on the couch asked.

"Dead," Hamp told him, and for one moment the old blinding rage and hate flashed through him. He wanted to snarl, How did you think she was after you left her with a month-old baby in a vermin-ridden hotel room without money, without friends, and sick?

Torgeson closed his eyes for a moment and then opened them to look at the ceiling. He said softly, "I got what I deserved, Cameron. I've paid for some of it these past two years. It's been hell just waiting for you to show up, never knowing when it would happen."

Hamp didn't say anything. There was nothing to say now, because it was over. He looked down at the foot of the couch, and then he looked at Bill Buckley by the door, and he wanted to get away. He needed a drink very badly.

Then Buckley came forward to stand by the couch and look down at the man. Hamp heard his voice as if from a long distance.

"Reckon he's gone," Buckley said.

When Hamp looked, Torgeson's head was again turned toward the wall. He was very still.

"Better get yourself a drink," Buckley advised.

Hamp left the room. He walked to the far end of the bar, which was empty at the moment, and he stood there, elbows on the wood, staring at nothing. When a bartender came toward him, he said stolidly, "Whisky."

When it came he drank it in one long draught and it had no effect on him other than a burning sensation in the stomach. He was conscious of the fact that men were staring at him all over the room as the word got around that he'd just killed a man.

The fat-faced bartender who waited on him was very deferential. He said, "Another one, mister?"

Hamp shook his head. Whisky did no good. It left him empty.

The bartender slapped at the bar with his rag as he moved past Hamp, and then he said hesitantly, "Reckon that was pretty fast shootin', mister." It was meant as flattery.

Hamp stared at the man, his jaws tight, and the bartender moved away hurriedly, saying no more.

Bill Buckley had a few words with a man whom Hamp took to be the local coroner, and then came over to the bar. He stood beside Hamp and ordered a drink, and then he drank it before saying anything. When he spoke he was looking at his own reflection in the mirror, not at Hamp. He said, "Helps a little sometimes to get it off your mind. Just tellin' somebody else about it."

Hamp glanced at him, put both hands around the little liquor glass on the bar in front of him, and said, "I had a younger sister, and we were very close. My father owned a small ranch fifty miles from Laramie in Wyoming. This man stopped by one day. He went by the name of Jensen in those days. Stayed for a month, doing odd jobs, and then he left. He had a way with women, and my sister left with him. They were never married. I located her nearly a year later in a run-down hotel in Frisco. She died the day after I found her. The baby died hours later. He was gone."

Bill Buckley was frowning into the mirror. "You caught up with him," he said after a few moments of silence, "and it's over. Are you figurin' on headin' back to Wyoming?"

Hamp shook his head. "My father died six months after she left," he said. "Nothing there any more."

He stood there against the bar, considering that fact, appalled by it. All along he'd had a goal and a purpose in life. He'd risen each morning to find the man; he'd gone to sleep each night with that thought in his mind, making his plans. Now it had come to an end, and he was empty.

For one horrible moment he almost wished he hadn't killed Jensen, so that he could have gone on chasing him indefinitely. There had been excitement and suspense and joy and disappointment connected with the chase. He had experienced emotions, and now he experienced nothing.

"Mormon's not a bad town," Bill Buckley was saying, "once you get used to the heat. Plenty o' work. Both borax outfits takin' on men."

Hamp didn't say anything. He still had a little money from the sale of the ranch after his father died, but he knew that he would have to get work sooner or later, not only to support himself, but to get his mind off other things.

"I'll think about it," he told Buckley. Then he pushed away from the bar and he saw a man standing to the left of the door as he went out, a man in a dark suit who watched him with cold, speculative eyes, a man with a narrow, pasty face and a thin slit of a mouth, the corners turned down. His eyes were small, set close together, colorless and hooded, and only when Hamp was outside did he know the man—not his name, not his identity, because he had never met the man in his life, but his profession: that of a cold-blooded, professional killer, his gun for hire to the best bidder.

The man in the dark suit had looked at Hamp with the same cool, wary detachment with which one gun sharp would look at another, wondering exactly how fast he was with a gun, weighing his own chances if someday he had to match draws with this man. A killer's mind worked that way. Hamp had run across many of them in the past two years.

Out on the street, Hamp turned left and walked toward the south end of town, not particularly knowing or

23

caring where he was going, and as he walked he found himself looking in over bat-wing doors, looking for a man—a man with blond hair like corn silk, and eyes of jade.

Chapter Three

The man across the table from Hamp was the blocky, broad-shouldered, blunt-nosed man he had seen come out of the Imperial Borax office the day before. Hamp noticed other things about him now, on closer inspection. He had reddish-brown hair and his teeth were strong, white, and even, but with a space between the two front ones. He spoke like a man who expected to have his way when he made a proposition. He said, "Name's Cordell—Lace Cordell. I run Imperial Borax. You've heard of us?"

Hamp picked up his coffee cup, nodding slightly as he did so. Cordell had entered the restaurant as Hamp was eating, took one look around the room, and then headed straight for Hamp's table in the corner. He had sat down without an invitation.

"Imperial," Cordell went on smoothly, confidently, "has been in business six months. We're a new outfit in the Valley, and a growing one. We could use a man of your caliber, Mr. Cameron."

"What's my caliber?" Hamp asked softly.

Lace Cordell looked at him sharply. He had amber-colored eyes, and his reddish hair was parted in the middle. He sat there with his hands clasped in front of him, and Hamp noticed the hands, big, powerful, but

24

uncalloused, the fingernails clean. Hamp had him tabbed as a man who got things done, who made his way in life, but not with his own sweat. Cordell didn't drive himself, but he knew how to drive lesser men.

"Heard a little about you last night," Cordell said evenly, "in the Piute Saloon."

Hamp had set the coffee cup down on the table. He leaned back in the chair now and felt in his coat pocket for a cigar. He said, "That right?"

Lace Cordell flipped a cigar out of his vest pocket and handed it to Hamp. It was a good cigar. Hamp smelled it and put it in his mouth, nodding his thanks.

Lace Cordell said, "If you figure on staying in Mormon, mister, there's a job with Imperial for you."

"What kind of a job?" Hamp asked curiously.

Cordell shrugged. "This is a new town, a new industry. We've picked up some rough characters and sometimes they get out of line. I need a man around to keep them from getting in each other's hair, and see that the borax gets out of the Valley."

Hamp nodded. "I'll think about it," he promised. "Haven't made any plans."

"You won't make any mistakes with Imperial," Cordell told him confidently. "In another year we'll own this Valley."

Thinking of Sheila Graham, Hamp looked at the man thoughtfully. He hadn't heard as yet that there was any particular rivalry between Valley Borax and the Imperial Company, but it was reasonable to assume that there would be. With two outfits in the Valley competing to get the borax out to the railhead and the big profits, there would naturally be competition. In a town like Mormon, filled with hard characters working for both companies, the rivalry could easily flare up into open warfare. Hamp had seen it happen before in mining towns, in range country.

"Don't be in too big a hurry to leave Mormon," Cordell advised. "Stop in and see us. We're paying top wages in this part of the country."

"That's nice," Hamp said, and there was still little interest in his voice.

Cordell glanced at him curiously. "You're not interested in money, mister?" he asked.

"No," Hamp said truthfully. He didn't know what he was interested in now. He was still empty, still trying to become acclimated eighteen hours after he'd killed Rob Jensen. He had no plans as yet, no hopes for the future.

Lace Cordell flicked ash from the tip of his cigar. "You're a queer one," he murmured.

"Am I?" Hamp said, and from the tone of voice he used he left little doubt that he didn't approve of the remark, and he didn't give a damn who knew it.

"All right," Lace Cordell said curtly. "If you want the job, stop in."

He left, and Hamp sat there with the cigar in his mouth, knowing that sooner or later he would have to do something. His money wouldn't last forever, and he had to get his feet back on solid ground, or forever be a lost man.

Leaving the restaurant, he walked under the shade of the overhead awnings. The heat was stifling. It made breathing difficult.

The train whistle sounded in the distance as the noonday train rolled in over Piute Pass and down across the open desert toward Mormon. Hamp headed for the station because there would be some activity there, and even now the hours were beginning to drag. He wanted, also, to have a closer look at the big borax rig he had seen rolling through town the previous day. The huge tandem wagons interested him.

Passing the hotel and walking down toward the Twenty Mule Saloon, he saw a man standing outside, his back against the wall, a man in black with a black hat. He was not a big man, but he wore exceptionally high-heeled boots to augment his size. His colorless eyes, hooded, close-set, watched Hamp thoughtfully as Hamp went by.

The same man had stood by the door of the Piute Saloon the previous night, watching Hamp leave after the killing of Jensen. The speculation had been in his eyes then, also.

Hamp looked at him, nodded briefly, impersonally, and kept going. He had the man labeled definitely now, a killer who would like to increase his own tawdry reputation if he could by shooting down another supposed killer. It was on nourishment such as this that a killer lived.

Moving down the walk, Hamp looked across the shimmering, heat-filled road into the cubbyhole of an office where Sheriff Bill Buckley sat, his chair tilted against the wall just inside the door. Buckley was looking straight at him, but Hamp couldn't tell if the man's eyes were opened or closed at the distance.

Buckley gave no sign that he'd seen him.

As he approached the Valley Borax office, the door opened, and the girl Hamp had seen inside the previous night came out. He had been looking toward the door as it opened, and his eyes met hers for a brief instant. He was surprised to learn that the color was violet. He had imagined they would be brown.

She was younger, too, than he had thought, probably twenty-one or twenty-two, and her hair was lighter in the daylight, almost a coppery color. He touched his hat brim to her, and she nodded and smiled faintly, recognizing him as a stranger in town. His reputation, achieved last night in the Piute Saloon, evidently had not yet penetrated the office of Valley Borax, and Hamp Cameron wondered if she would still smile at him when she knew.

At the railroad station he stood under the shade of the wooden awning and watched a dozen or so languid, flushed passengers step down from the cars and head immediately for the nearest saloon for a cooling drink.

He watched the engineer eventually maneuver an empty boxcar onto the siding, where two borax wagons stood. The huge wagons had been unloaded and the sacks of borax piled on the loading platform. On the high wooden sides of each wagon were painted the words "Valley Borax."

The mules had been unhooked from the wagons and probably taken to the Valley Company yard in town. A pair of worn boots protruded from beneath the lead wagon, and Hamp strolled that way leisurely, feeling the full glare of the sun again as he came out from under the awning.

As he moved around to have a look at the water tank, the man under the wagon, evidently one of the drivers or a swamper, poked his head out, blinking in the bright sunshine. He was a stubby little man with a round head, face red as a beet, a flattened stub of a nose, and twinkling blue eyes.

Rubbing his jaw with a grimy hand, he said to Hamp jocularly, "Ain't figurin' on drivin' one o' these rigs, now, are you, mister?"

Hamp shook his head. He squatted down in front of the man. He said, "They hard to handle?"

"Would be," the little man grinned, "if it weren't fer them damn mules. Smarter than most people, them mules, mister. They handle the load. I sit up on the seat or ride one o' the wheelers, an' let 'em run."

"Ten spans of mules," Hamp said. "You need that many?"

"If you seen some o' the road in the Valley," the driver chuckled, "you wouldn't ask that question, mister." He was staring at Hamp curiously, and then he said, "Ain't you the feller—" He stopped, rubbed his jaw some more, and finished lamely, "Wasn't you in the Piute Saloon last night when that shootin' was goin' on?"

"I was in the shooting," Hamp told him. "It get any hotter in the Valley than it is around here?"

The Valley Borax driver grinned. "Mister," he said, "I seen it so hot out at Furnace Creek that the water was boilin' in my canteen."

"That right?" Hamp grinned.

The short man crossed himself. "Stubby McCoy never lied in his life," he stated blandly, "exceptin' when he was under the influence o' liquor, an' then he may have exaggerated a bit."

Hamp went off on a new tack, knowing he had a man here who liked to talk. He said casually, "This new Imperial outfit giving you boys trouble?"

Stubby McCoy frowned. "Not yet," he admitted, "but I ain't likin' that Cordell feller too much. He's slick an' he's after big money."

"Should be plenty of borax in the Valley for both outfits," Hamp observed.

"Plenty o' borax an' new deposits bein' found in the ranges along the Valley," Stubby said, "but the more o' the stuff goes out, the lower the price gets. Borax Charlie Graham, who started the whole business, figured he could snake borax out o' Death Valley for a cent a pound an' sell it at the railhead fer ten. With two an' maybe more outfits in the business, that ten-cent-a-pound price ain't holdin'. Down to nine now, an' it'll go lower."

"Still a big profit," Hamp stated.

"Big enough fer Miss Sheila," Stubby said, "but the way I'm thinkin', Lace Cordell an' his Imperial outfit would like to see it bigger. Reckon he'd like it a lot better, too, if there was only one borax company bringin' the stuff out. Then he could name his own price to the buyers an' let 'em holler if they wouldn't pay it."

Hamp thought about that. It was a good setup for a man with the money and the ruthlessness he suspected in Lace Cordell. If Cordell could buy or force Valley

Borax out of business, he would be king of Death Valley, in a position to make himself a vast fortune with borax buyers on the outside clamoring for more and more of the stuff, willing to pay high prices to get it.

"Cordell made an offer for the company first week he landed in Mormon," Stubby McCoy was saying. "Miss Sheila an' Stuart Fleming turned him down."

Hamp remembered the blond-haired man he'd seen talking with Sheila Graham in the office last night. He said, "Fleming superintendent of Valley Borax?"

"There's a man," Stub McCoy said admiringly. "Never think he was a damned Easterner. Regular as all hell."

"One of Borax Charlie Graham's men?" Hamp asked curiously.

Stub shook his head. "Fleming come to Mormon right after Charlie kicked out with sunstroke. Reckon Miss Sheila needed a good man to keep the wheels rollin', an' Stuart Fleming fit the glove. Even the Chinamen scoopin' up the borax out at the reduction plant like him. They work like hell whenever he comes in sight."

Hamp looked at the wagon under which Stub McCoy was still sitting. He said, "You handle the same rig all the way out to the plant and back?"

"Hell, no." McCoy grinned. "My run is out to Devil's Hole Spring an' back. We got rotatin' drivers, pickin' up the wagons, rollin' 'em on. My route ain't no cinch, though. Sixteen miles out to Devil's Hole, an' then I pick up full loads an' move 'em in here. Six miles o' that route is over rock salt, hard as iron, an' it bounces the insides out of a man."

Both men heard the rumbling sound, then, as another borax rig rolled out around the station and headed toward the loading platform, the ten spans of mules strung out, stepping lively, the driver riding the near wheeler, cracking his long whip.

Hamp noticed how, as they swung and moved toward the platform, the third team from the wagon moved in the opposite direction from the lead animals, stepping sideways very nimbly, thus preventing the rig from overturning and making a clean, easy swing.

"Them pointers are a good pair," Stub McCoy said admiringly as he came from underneath the wagon to watch. "They been trained."

"One of your rigs?" Hamp asked him.

"Imperial," Stub McCoy murmured, "an' it looks like trouble. That's Red Doran handlin' that jerk line. He an' me ain't particular friends. I near upset his rig week ago comin' out through Wind Gap."

The Imperial wagons were brought to a stop, both men working the brakes, the driver on the wheeler applying his brake by means of a rope that he yanked. He was a big fellow, flaming red hair, freckled face. He wore a faded gray flannel shirt, a tattered flat-crowned hat, and high boots, and from the way he walked Hamp could sense that he meant to make trouble.

Stub McCoy was rubbing his hands on his worn Levis. He was a head shorter than Doran, the Imperial man, but a fighter, and unafraid.

Doran came up, a tough smile on his face. He said evenly, "McCoy, git that damned rig out o' there. I'm unloadin'."

Stub McCoy spat. "I'll put it on my back," he said. "I'll walk off with it—eight ton o' wood an' iron. Go jump off Pilot Peak, Red."

The Imperial driver tightened his belt. His swamper, a shorter man with sloping shoulders and a drooping mustache, came around the water tank, grinning. Doran glanced at Hamp standing by, a cigar in his mouth, legs spread slightly, hands behind his back, listening, watching calmly.

"Don't care how you move these dump wagons," Doran told him, "but I want 'em moved, pronto."

"Keep your shirt on," Stub McCoy advised. "If you can't wait till we bring a few teams out from our yard, you kin hook some o' yore own animals in an' move it yourself."

Red Doran's grin broadened. "Lace Cordell heard Imperial mules was haulin' Valley wagons an' he'd cut my heart out. Now git movin', McCoy, an' run some o' yore damned animals out here."

"Don't move no wagons," McCoy told him, "till I git orders from Fleming. You go see Fleming, Red."

The grin left Doran's wide, tough face. "I been out in this sun, McCoy," he rasped, "since six o'clock this mornin'. I ain't standin' here waitin' while you work yore mouth. Now git to hell over to yore yard an' bring them mules here."

"Fleming's yore man," Stub McCoy told him.

Red Doran was standing six feet away. He didn't move, but he spat deliberately across the tip of McCoy's boot. The insult was too much for the stubby man. McCoy hinged forward, cursing savagely, and Doran, who had been waiting for the move, lashed out with a hard right fist that caught the Valley driver on the side of the jaw, dropping him to the ground.

The swamper with Doran said tersely, "Give it to him, Red."

Red Doran drew back his boot to kick at McCoy as he started to get up, shaking his head stupidly, and then Hamp Cameron said easily, "Reckon that's enough, mister."

Doran didn't kick. He looked Hamp over from head to foot, then said softly, "An' who the hell is this, now?"

Hamp tilted the cigar upward with his teeth. He still stood with his hands behind his back and his legs spread.

"Don't kick him," he said.

Red Doran grinned. "Maybe you're right, mister." He chuckled. "He's standin' up now, anyway."

Stub McCoy had raised himself to his feet and was looking around dazedly, fists balled. Doran stepped up and smashed him in the mouth with a swinging left-hand blow, driving him back up against the front wheel of the Valley wagon. Blood started to trickle down McCoy's chin. He cursed and lunged forward with his short arms, trying to hit his man, but he was no match for the taller, heavier Doran, and Doran hit him a half-dozen times, backing him against the wagon again.

Hamp tossed the cigar away, slipped out of his coat almost in one motion, and came up behind Doran. Grasping the redhead by the shoulder, he spun him around with his left hand, and then drove his right deep into the Imperial driver's stomach.

Doran's breath belched out. Mouth open, he stumbled away, holding his stomach, and Hamp waited until he'd recovered, giving him full opportunity to continue the fight or walk away from it. Doran chose the former course.

"Reckon you walked into a lickin', mister," he panted when he had recovered somewhat, and he drove in, big fists swinging, aiming for Hamp's head.

Hamp made no effort to avoid him. He stepped in, driving hard, vicious blows into Doran's body, and then working them up into the redhead's face, and he kept moving forward as he punched, the fury of his attack literally sweeping Doran off his feet. A hard right smash to the jaw dropped Doran to his knees, the blood spouting from his nose and cut lips. He got up slowly, plenty of fight in him, Hamp could see, but a little wary.

Stub McCoy, who had recovered now, said to Hamp, "Let me work on him now, mister."

Hamp shook his head, and then McCoy turned on Doran's swamper.

"How about it, friend?" he asked, and then he swung his fist at the Imperial man's head, whooped, and piled on top of him.

Doran came in again, circling Hamp in a half crouch. Hamp saw Stub McCoy and the Imperial swamper rolling on the ground, punching at each other, and then Doran lunged in, trying to grapple with Hamp this time and throw him to the ground.

Hamp let him close in, and then he came up hard with his left fist, driving it into Doran's neck. The redhead gagged as he staggered back, and then Hamp hit him one solid blow to the side of the jaw, and the fight was over. Doran stretched out on the sand, arms spread.

Stub McCoy and the Imperial swamper were still rolling on the ground, punching each other. Hamp walked over and lifted McCoy to his feet, the little man still swinging happily.

"That's enough." Hamp smiled.

The swamper got to his feet, cursing, and then he looked down at Red Doran dumbly. Stub McCoy stared at him, too, and then walked around to the rear of the water tank, drew a pailful of water, and came back to throw it across Doran's face.

The redhead sat up, spluttering. He shook his head several times, and then daubed at his cut mouth with a dirty handkerchief. Looking at Hamp, he said slowly, "Reckon you're buckin' a pretty big outfit, mister. Better make sure you're on the right side."

Hamp picked up his coat and dusted it off before putting it on. He said, "I'm not picking any side, Red."

"Mister," the Imperial driver told him significantly, "you already picked your side. Just remember that."

He got up, then, and walked to his mules, his swamper following him. Hamp watched him mount the near wheeler and then crack his whip. The twenty mules surged forward, and Doran rolled the rig a hundred yards past the siding into the shade of a long, low warehouse.

Stub McCoy said thoughtfully, "Reckon I owe you a drink, mister, fer steppin' in there. That Doran is a tough one, an' I'm hopin' you ain't got yourself into trouble by takin' my part."

"I'll worry about it," Hamp said.

McCoy went back to the water tank for another pail of water and a tin cup. Both men drank deeply, the energy they'd used up in the fight having drained them of moisture.

"You drink it," McCoy said, "till it comes out o' the ears, an' then you want more."

Hamp heard footsteps crunching the sand behind him, and when he turned his head he saw Stuart Fleming coming up. The Valley Borax superintendent smiled and lifted a hand to them. He said curiously to McCoy, noting the puffed lips and the swelling right eye, "Trouble out here, Stub?"

Stub McCoy explained, nodding toward the Imperial rig parked by the warehouse. They could see Red Doran over there, stripped to the waist in the shade now, washing his face and arms in a bucket of water he'd drawn from the tank.

"This feller," Stub nodded toward Hamp, "walked into it."

Stuart Fleming's eyes were turquoise, and with that square chin and the blond, wavy hair, he was a handsome man. It was his manner, however, Hamp could see, that captivated people. The man had background and education, and yet he was regular. He didn't seem to drive men, but the chances were that he got more out of them than Lace Cordell, who used the mailed fist.

"We're obliged to you," Fleming said cordially, extending his hand. "I don't like to see these altercations between our drivers, but I suppose they must happen. You're new in this town?"

"Came in yesterday," Hamp told him. He shook the man's hand, a little surprised at the strength of the handshake. "Hamp Cameron," he said.

"Stuart Fleming," the Valley Borax man said.

"This feller," Stub McCoy nodded toward Hamp, anxious to impart information, "had that little trouble in the Piute Saloon last night. Reckon you heard about it, Mr. Fleming."

Stuart Fleming's blue-green eyes lifted a little with interest, and Hamp could see from the expression on his face that he'd assumed some town tough had been involved in the shooting. His remark, however, was typical of the man. He said, "An unfortunate incident, Mr. Cameron."

He refrained from asking any questions, and Hamp respected him for that. Fleming said thoughtfully, "Staying in Mormon, Mr. Cameron?"

Hamp shrugged. "Hard to say," he stated.

"Booming town." Fleming smiled. "Plenty of work for good men, and not too bad when you get used to the heat."

Hamp noticed that he didn't offer him a job, as had Lace Cordell. Evidently Fleming wasn't hiring men who were quick and deadly with a gun, and capable with their fists.

"I like cooler places," Hamp told him, and they let the matter drop there. A few minutes later, walking back to town, Hamp tried to analyze his feelings about Stuart Fleming. The Valley Borax superintendent was nice, very nice, and almost too nice, and that, Hamp decided, was the flaw in him. A man could be decent up to a point. Men mistrusted women who went out of their way to be friendly, and the same principle could apply to other men.

Passing again the Twenty Mule Saloon, Hamp saw the man in the dark suit still lounging in the same place, a toothpick in his mouth, hands in his pockets, one leg crossed, and a shoulder against the doorpost. He was watching Hamp reflectively as he came up, and in his lusterless eyes was that same question.

The pearl handle of a pistol protruded from a black leather holster on the man's left side. He was a left-handed man, which would give him an unorthodox draw.

Again Hamp nodded faintly to him, a slow smile playing around the corners of his mouth as he went by, but after he had passed the man the smile disappeared and he frowned. Less than twenty-four hours before he'd been involved in gun play. He didn't want any more, particularly a senseless gun duel based upon a man's warped and twisted vanity.

Chapter Four

At eight o'clock that night Hamp put on a clean shirt after shaving and washing. He had a small bruise on his right cheekbone, the only mark of the encounter with Red Doran.

He'd had his supper in the restaurant adjoining the hotel, and he'd come back to the room after eating, the restlessness running through him again. The fight with Doran had helped a little, having taken some of the excess energy from him, and he realized now that his only salvation lay in taking hold of something, somewhere, having a purpose in life again.

He found himself thinking about Sheila Graham and Stuart Fleming, wondering if their relationship was more than a business one. He wouldn't have blamed the girl if she'd fallen for Fleming. In a town like Mormon there wouldn't be too many men with his looks, personality, and ability, and Sheila Graham was young, and she needed help.

Strapping on his gun belt, Hamp slipped into his coat and stepped out into the corridor. As he came out into the lobby he was surprised to find Miss Graham just stepping away from the desk, a batch of mail in her hands. It was the first intimation he'd had that the hotel clerk served, also, as the local postmaster.

As the girl moved toward the door, Hamp stepped up quickly to hold it open for her. She smiled and nodded her thanks as she passed through, and Hamp said to her, "It ever cool off out this way?"

"We have ideal weather in midwinter," Sheila Graham told him. They both stopped outside on the walk, and Hamp could see her face clearly in the yellow light from the lamps in the lobby. She was smiling at him, and again he found himself wondering how close she was to Stuart Fleming, and hoping they were no more than business associates.

"If a man could live through the summer," Hamp observed, "he might be able to enjoy the winter."

"Summer's nearly over," Miss Graham smiled. "We've just started to run borax out of the Valley the past few weeks' There is no work done during the real hot months."

Hamp looked at her. "Unusual finding a woman in a business like this," he observed.

Sheila Graham shrugged a little. "I like it," she said simply. "Death Valley is beautiful for a good part of the year. Have you ever seen desert holly, or creosote bushes in bloom?"

"No," Hamp said.

"I used to ride on top of my father's borax wagons when I was quite young," the girl went on, "the first borax ever taken out of Death Valley. At sunset you could see the mountains changing color, and the heavy shadows crawling across the valley floor. In the proper season the Valley is one of the most beautiful spots in America."

"Reckon I'll have to take a ride out before I leave," Hamp murmured.

"You're a stranger in Mormon," Sheila said. "Are you looking for work?"

Hamp had his hat in his hand now, and he turned it around in his fingers before answering. Then he said, "Not yet. Have to work out a few things first."

"We'll be hiring men during the winter months," Sheila said. "If you're looking for work, you might stop in and see us at Valley Borax."

"Obliged," Hamp said, and he wondered why it was that Stuart Fleming, the superintendent, hadn't made him an offer if the company was taking on help.

"The borax industry is still growing," Sheila told him. "There's a tremendous demand for it, and we're anxious

41

to sign up men who will want to grow with us.

"Reckon I'll think about it," Hamp said.

After she left, he stood on the walk for some time, not sure which way to go, and then he crossed the road and stepped into the Death Valley Saloon, one of the larger saloons in town. The Piute Saloon was a few doors below, but he did not want to go in there.

At the bar he spotted Sheriff Bill Buckley talking with Stuart Fleming. Buckley lifted a finger to him, and then motioned for him to come over for a drink. Fleming smiled at him and took the cigar from his mouth to look at it.

Buckley said thoughtfully, "Still around, are you, Cameron?"

"No rush leaving," Hamp told him.

"You ought to ride out into the Valley before you leave," Stuart Fleming told him. "Lowest spot in the United States. If you think it's hot in Mormon, wait till you enter the Valley."

"I might do that." Hamp smiled faintly. He saw Lace Cordell, head man of Imperial Borax, come in through the doors, walking with that peculiar, heavy-footed roll. The man's amber eyes moved to the three at the bar. Hamp saw him frown a little, and then drop down at one of the card tables, where he signaled a waiter for a drink.

It was evident that the Death Valley Saloon was head-quarters for the borax industry. Stub McCoy, the little Valley driver, entered a few moments after Cordell, waved a cheery hand to Hamp and Stuart Fleming at the bar, and then joined other men at the far end of the room, obviously Valley employees.

Hamp said to Fleming, "How far is your reduction plant from Mormon?"

"Hundred and sixty-odd miles," the superintendent stated. "Rough all the way. Charlie Graham, I understand, laid out the road, and it's been improved over the bad spots, but it still isn't a first class road."

"Imperial use it, also?" Hamp wanted to know.

Fleming nodded. He was smoking a cigar, and he looked at the cigar now before speaking.

"No one owns the right of way," he explained. "Cordell has built his stations not too far from ours. Of course, we have the big advantage because we were on the ground first and we've built around most of the water holes."

"That means," Hamp murmured, "that Imperial has to carry a good deal of its water out to the way stations."

Stuart Fleming nodded again. "They're forced to carry extra water on their loads," he explained, "to keep the water barrels at their stations filled. We load borax."

Hamp put both elbows on the bar and looked into the mirror. He was aware of the fact that Sheriff Buckley was listening in on this conversation, although he was taking no part in it.

"That could mean," Hamp observed casually, "that in the long run the outfit controlling the best water holes can force out the company hauling its own water."

Stuart Fleming looked at him in the mirror as he flicked ash from his cigar. "It could mean that," he admitted.

43

"Did Cordell know that when he set up his borax outfit?" Hamp asked.

Fleming smiled, but Hamp noticed that there was a glint in his turquoise eyes, and he had the feeling that the man was not always as friendly, as pleasant and agreeable as he pretended to be.

"Ask him," Fleming said simply.

Hamp turned to lean his elbows on the bar now, and he looked across the room at Lace Cordell at the card table. He caught the Imperial Borax man glancing at him. Cordell gave him a long, searching look, and then put his head down to look at his cards.

That was when the man in black came through the bat-wing doors. He walked unhurriedly into the room, his hands in his pockets, coat drawn back, revealing the gun on his left hip. His colorless, hooded eyes moved along the bar, coming to rest on Hamp, who was facing him directly. The eyes paused for a moment and then moved on again, and he walked past the table at which Lace Cordell sat.

Hamp saw Cordell glance up at the man. Something may have passed between them, but neither man nodded or gave any indication that they knew each other, and yet Hamp was positive that they did. He felt the agitation again in the pit of his stomach, and then he turned and said to Bill Buckley, "Who was that man walked in, Sheriff?"

Buckley rubbed his prow of a nose. "Goes by the name of Merle Wynant," he said. "Landed in Mormon a week ago. A cold fish, if I've ever seen one."

"To me," Stuart Fleming put in idly, "he'd pass as a

44

professional gun thrower."

"What would a gun hand be doing in Mormon?" Hamp asked.

Fleming only shrugged, but Bill Buckley said casually, "Reckon we get all kinds in this town, Cameron. Lot of 'em come this way because the law gets too hot for 'em in other places."

"And it's not hot here?" Hamp smiled.

"Not till they get out o' line," Bill Buckley told him quietly. He walked off, and Hamp watched him go, wondering again how tough the man was. He heard Stuart Fleming say at his elbow:

"You good at stud poker, Mr. Cameron?"

"Let's find out," Hamp invited.

Fleming brought over two other men and they found a corner table that was unoccupied. As Hamp was sitting down he saw the small man in black still at the bar, not drinking, just standing there, his eyes moving, always moving. The man watched Hamp sit down, and then he looked away, and soon his eyes roved back again, restless and shifting.

After a while he moved away from the bar and took a position not more than twenty feet from the table at which Hamp sat. He pretended to be watching a poker game nearby, but constantly Hamp caught him glancing in their direction. There was never any expression in the man's face. It was a dead face, but the eyes were alive now. His eyes were like two pieces of ice with match light showing behind them.

After the third hand, which Hamp won with two pairs, a sweaty-faced, lank man in a faded blue flannel shirt pushed his way around the tables and came tip to the chair where Stuart Fleming sat. The lank man said tersely, "Been lookin' for you, Mr. Fleming. Reckon we got some trouble out at Devil's Hole Spring, Number Nine station."

Stuart Fleming leaned back in the chair, smiling, but Hamp saw his eyes narrowing. "What kind of trouble, Jim?" he asked pleasantly.

"Sam Corwin an' me brought our rig into Devil's Hole station at noon today." The lank man scowled. "Found both attendants gone, an' the mules gone. When we watered our animals at the spring, five of 'em went crazy an' died. Rig's still out there. I come in here on one o' the wheelers."

Hamp watched Stuart Fleming's face. The smile was gone, but there was no particular tension in his face. It was still pleasant and relaxed, but his eyes seemed to have changed color. They were almost blue now, and they had receded into his head. He said quietly, "Would you say that water hole had been poisoned, Jim?"

"Mules don't drop dead from good water," Jim said.

"You didn't see the attendants?" Fleming went on.

"Skipped," Jim told him. "Reckon they're clean gone from the Valley."

Hamp had been shuffling the cards, preparing to deal, but he held up the deal now with Stuart Fleming engaged, and he continued to shuffle the cards, and then he glanced left in the direction of Lace Cordell.

The owner of Imperial Borax was sitting back in his chair, staring at the cards in his hand. Then he picked up a half-empty liquor glass and downed the contents, still

46

not looking in their direction.

Stuart Fleming was saying to the driver, "Send Stub McCoy out with fresh mules to bring the rig in. See if you can get that spring cleaned out so that it can be ready for the next outfit going through. I'll have two new attendants here sometime tomorrow and we'll get rolling again."

The lank driver nodded and left them. Hamp saw him corner Stubby McCoy, the squat driver, and then both men left, talking excitedly. Stuart Fleming sat with his hands flat on the table, staring straight ahead of him, and Hamp said, "Trouble?"

"You heard it." Fleming smiled faintly. "Poisoning water holes is bad business in this country."

"Who would do it?" Hamp asked him.

He had little doubt who had bought off or chased off the two Valley Borax employees at Devil's Hole station and then poisoned the spring. A borax war had been in the offing for some time, and Lace Cordell and his Imperial outfit had fired the first shot. First it would be nuisance attacks like this, only a few mules killed, a load of borax delayed on its way to Mormon. Later, it would flare up into open warfare with raids on the giant wagons, cargoes destroyed, hired gun hands brought in, and then one or the other of the big companies would have to quit the Valley.

It was going to be a fight between two utterly different characters—the tough, ruthless Lace Cordell, who said what he thought and didn't give a damn for anyone, and the cool, smiling Stuart Fleming, who had proved himself efficient and likable as the Valley Borax superintendent, but still hadn't proved that he had the guts for the job. Fleming was Sheila Graham's ace card. Valley Borax lived or died according to his actions.

"I'll find out who did it," Fleming was saying. "Shall we continue the game, Mr. Cameron?"

Hamp dealt the cards, a slight frown on his face. Fleming was smiling again, bland and cool and pleasant. There had been no particular threat in his voice. He knew, as well as Hamp, that the man responsible for the raid on the station sat less than fifteen feet from him. No man in Mormon, except a crank or a lunatic, would poison a water hole without reason. Lace Cordell had his reasons, and good ones. Fleming knew it, and Fleming continued to play stud poker.

Hamp started to wonder if perhaps he'd mistaken the man. He'd had the feeling when first meeting Fleming that the blond man had something underneath the smooth, polished exterior. Possibly he'd been wrong, and if he was, it meant that Sheila Graham's Valley Borax would go under.

He tried to learn something of the man from his poker playing, remembering that Rob Jensen, with whom he'd played in the bunkhouse of his father's ranch, had been a plunger, gambling all on the turn of a single card, caring little for the consequences.

Stuart Fleming played poker stolidly, giving each card its full value, taking no chances. He was careful, rather than cautious, and he would not be bluffed. Hamp could make much or nothing out of these facts. A cautious man or a careful man could be a man afraid.

Leaning back in his chair after dealing the cards,

Hamp looked toward the bar at the man Merle Wynant, whom he'd taken to be a professional killer. If Wynant were acquainted with Lace Cordell, it could be that Cordell had hired his gun for this coming fight, just as Cordell had tried to hire him, Hamp Cameron, who had just proved himself in a gun fight. Cordell was hiring guns, not men.

Stuart Fleming played a few more hands, and then excused himself politely and dropped out of the game. The bat-wing door was still swinging where Fleming had gone out when a man came up behind the vacant chair and said softly, "Mind if I sit in?"

When Hamp looked up, he looked into the dull, ice-like eyes of Merle Wynant.

Chapter Five

The other two men at the table with Hamp, a shop-keeper by the name of King and the local livery-stable man, had no objections. Hamp looked at the cards in his hand and nodded briefly. Wynant took a seat to his left, and he sat there with his hands folded in front of him, looking down at the table, waiting until this hand was played out and he would be dealt in.

Hamp watched him take a cigar out of his pocket, bite off the end, and put it in his mouth. Glancing once again in Lace Cordell's direction, Hamp caught him with a small frown on his face. Cordell was looking at Merle Wynant, disapproval on his wide, blunt-nosed face. Evidently Cordell knew, also, why his gun hand was sitting in at the game, and did not like it.

49

They're all alike, Hamp thought idly. They can't sleep if they think there's a man in town who can throw lead faster than themselves.

Wynant was curious, and he had to find out. It was burning in him, giving him no rest. The blood lust was upon him, and he would have no peace until he'd satisfied his morbid curiosity. Hamp found himself wondering how the gunman would bring about the showdown. He didn't want it, himself, but he realized now that this was one of the reasons he had not already bought his ticket out of Mormon. He could not run when another man was maneuvering for a showdown.

Dealing Wynant a hand, he watched the man's play. The killer was a cool gambler. He took his chances, more so than had Stuart Fleming, but, unlike Fleming, he could be bluffed.

Hamp tried it with a pair of tens, and he forced Wynant out of the bidding, positive the gunman had better cards than his own. He tried it again ten minutes later with nothing in his hand at all, and again Merle Wynant dropped out, and Hamp filed this information away for fixture reference. The man who could be bluffed at poker was not a full man, not a complete man. There was a hole in him.

They played silently, speaking only to ask for cards or to raise bids, and even then many times making these requests with finger motions or nods of the head. Not particularly wanting to, Hamp started to win quite steadily. Luck ran the way of the disinterested, the way it usually did, and his pile of chips continued to rise. He noticed Wynant glancing at him quite often now, a thin smile beginning to play around the corners of his mouth, and he fancied he knew how the killer would steer his actions.

It was old and hackneyed, and yet Hamp remembered, ironically, that a man killed this way was just as dead as a man who met death in a more complex situation.

After Hamp won another pot, his third in succession, Merle Wynant said softly, casually, "Luck runnin' your way, mister."

"That's so," Hamp agreed. He shuffled the cards and looked straight at the man, and it was the first time he'd done so at close range. What he saw shocked him. Actually, this killer was a little rat of a man who had discovered, perhaps by accident, that he was very fast with a six-gun. He'd spent hundreds of hours practicing his draw and shooting at tin cans, and then he'd killed his first man. After that it had been easier, because his reputation had gone on ahead of him, making him bigger and more dangerous than he was, enervating better men so that they went down before his smoking gun.

Since then he'd lived on blood, his vanity reaching the bursting point, but underneath he was still the weak little man, physically, who had been half frightened to death before his first killing. That first killing, however, had made him different, just as his, Hamp's, killing of Rob Jensen had affected him. The evil little worm had crawled around inside his head, transforming him into a deadly killer.

Merle Wynant said, "Reckon you've played a lot o' stud poker, mister."

"That's so." Hamp smiled faintly. The stage was being set now, one piece at a time. A word here and a word there, a look, a gesture, and then the soft but deadly accusation, and a man had to draw his gun or forever walk with his head down.

Suddenly Hamp knew how he would handle the man; he knew, too, that his own moment of terrible danger was over. He wasn't going the way of Merle Wynant. He sat back more relaxed in the chair.

The shopkeeper, King, who had seen the way the game was going, suddenly decided that he had an appointment on the other side of town. Sliding back his chair, he got up, excused himself, and left. The third man in the game had not yet become aware of the fact that he was sitting close to a powder keg. He was a roly-poly little man by the name of Jack Dawes, very cheerful, and absorbed in the game.

Dawes won a pot, and then Hamp drew two pair on the next deal, kings and eights. He added another eight, giving him a full house, and then he sat back, folded his cards, and placed them face down on the table, prepared to bid.

To his left Merle Wynant had cast off two cards and drawn two, and now was watching Hamp carefully. He'd either had three of a kind or one pair, hoping to make it two. In either case Hamp's full house had him beaten, but Wynant wouldn't know about that full house. The little gunman had been bluffed before and he knew it. Now with good cards in his hands he would stay in the game, thinking Hamp had tried to fill a straight and missed, and was now bluffing. Wynant wouldn't be very happy when he saw the cards in Hamp's hands.

Hamp raised the bid; Jack Dawes dropped out, and Merle Wynant lifted it again. Hamp hesitated as if not sure of himself, and then added more chips to the pot, raising it another ten dollars. Wynant met the bid and lifted it again, his eyes narrowed now, leaning forward a little.

Dawes said, "Getting hot, gentlemen."

Neither Hamp nor Wynant spoke. The pot was up to nearly a hundred dollars, the biggest pot of the game thus far, and Hamp could see that Wynant wanted to win it very badly. His disappointment would undoubtedly bring the issue to a head.

Hamp pushed his chair back very slightly and got his feet settled beneath him, ready to make his move. Wynant saw the next bid and placed his cards face up on the table. He had three aces, a jack, and a queen, and he was smiling thinly as he looked at Hamp.

Hamp set down the full house—three eights and a pair of kings—and without a word raked in the pot.

The little gunman was silent for one moment, and then he said slowly, significantly, "Man has to know how to handle cards to deal himself a hand like that."

Hamp had been the dealer on the pot, and the statement was as blunt as Wynant could make it. Little Jack Dawes, staring at him, let his jaw fall, and his eyes moved to Hamp. It was Hamp's bid, and Hamp suddenly went into action.

Without a moment's warning he was on his feet, lunging at Merle Wynant, grabbing him by the coat front and jerking him to his feet. The move was totally unexpected, and Wynant let out a short yelp of astonishment.

Hamp spun him, drove him back against the wall, pinned him there with one big hand, and then slashed his free hand back and forth across the little man's face, the slaps resounding through the whole saloon.

Wynant cursed futilely and tried to bring his gun out of the holster, but Hamp grabbed his gun hand just as his fingers closed on the pearl handle of the gun. He ripped Wynant's hand away, lifted the gun himself, and tossed it away, and then he continued to slap the little man's face. He used his open hand in deliberate insult, but they were hard, swinging blows, reddening Wynant's face, bringing tears of rage, pain, and humiliation to his eyes.

He cursed and wriggled frantically to break loose, but he was no match for Hamp, and Hamp continued to slap him, slapping away all the pride and the vanity of the man, leaving him a helpless wreck when he'd finished.

It was brutal and it was painful. It was intended to drive the killer's conceit from the man, and when Hamp finally stepped back and let Wynant stumble away blindly, he knew that to a point he had succeeded. Wynant would never again face him openly with a gun. The man would strike from ambush like a rattler; he might even spend a lifetime looking for the chance to shoot his tormentor in the back, but he would never come from the front again. His spirit had been broken.

The big crowd in the Twenty Mule Saloon had watched silently, no one making a move to interfere. Wynant, holding his red face, went out through the bat-wing doors, and Hamp walked back to the card table, picked up his chips, and headed for the bar to cash them.

He had to walk past Lace Cordell's table to reach the bar, and Cordell was sitting back in his chair, a definite frown on his face now, convincing Hamp that Merle Wynant had been his man. Cordell wasn't too pleased to see his gun thrower, whom he'd hired as a big stick in this coming war, manhandled.

Cordell was a big man, too, and a fighter, if Hamp could judge a man. Merle Wynant's beating reflected to some measure upon himself, and while he did not openly wish to establish a connection between himself and Wynant, Hamp could see that he was having a hard time just dismissing the matter.

As Hamp walked past his chair, Cordell said evenly, "Reckon you didn't pick on too big a man now, did you, Cameron?"

Hamp stopped and he stood there with the chips stacked in his hands. He was smiling, but his gray eyes were a shade lighter. He said softly, "Who dealt you in, Cordell?"

"I made a statement of fact," Lace Cordell growled. He made no move to get up, and Hamp knew that it would not come to a head now, but he had displeased Cordell, and he had stood up against the man, and sooner or later their differences would have to be set-tled.

Hamp smiled down at him. He said nothing, but as he

continued on his way he saw the red come into Cordell's wide face, and his nostrils dilate. That smile had been a deliberate insult.

Walking to the bar, Hamp had one of the bartenders cash his chips. He had won a little over two hundred dollars in this game.

A man stepped up to the bar behind him and handed the bartender Wynant's gun for safekeeping. The bartender placed it on a shelf behind him, and he said to Hamp, significantly, "I'd walk careful, mister, if I was you."

"Aim to," Hamp said.

He had a drink at the bar, and he heard the talk start up in the room again. Card games that had been temporarily suspended got under way again. Jack Dawes, who had remained at his table when Hamp went after Wynant, came over to the bar, taking an open space next to Hamp. As he ordered his drink he said carefully, "Reckon that feller won't make any remarks to you, Mr. Cameron."

Hamp just shrugged. He was lighting up a cigar, looking around the room, wondering where Stuart Fleming had gone, and wondering what he intended to do to counteract the first blow by Imperial Borax.

"Funny thing," Dawes went on, "a little feller like that trying to pick a fight."

"With a gun in the hand," Hamp observed, "everybody's about equal."

Pushing away from the bar, he moved out through the doors and stood on the porch. It was still hot and close, but not as bad as it had been during the day.

A rider moved past the front of the saloon, his horse kicking up the alkali dust, and the particles hung in the still air, glittering in the light from the lamps inside. A man angled across the street from the direction of the hotel, passing through the dust, and Hamp recognized the long gaunt frame of Sheriff Bill Buckley.

Buckley came up on the walk, pausing on the steps below Hamp, looking up at him. He said thoughtfully, "So you had it out with this Wynant chap."

Hamp nodded and took the cigar from his mouth to look at it.

"Glad it wasn't with guns," Buckley grunted. "Glad for you, too, Cameron."

"He wouldn't have killed me," Hamp said.

Bill Buckley looked at him steadily. "Reckon I didn't mean that," he stated quietly.

Hamp smiled a little.

"Always better to use your fists on a man," Buckley went on slowly. "Better for him, an' a hell of a lot better for you."

"I know it," Hamp agreed.

"An' now there's more hell to pay," Bill Buckley growled, "an' it won't be settled with fists the way I'm thinkin'. You heard o' the trouble out at Devil's Hole Spring, the Valley Borax station?"

"Heard it." Hamp nodded. He was wondering if Stuart Fleming had run immediately to the Sheriff with his troubles.

"Fleming wants to know if I can do anything about it." Buckley shook his head in disgust. "Water hole's been poisoned an' he lost some mules. His attendants

57

skipped the country. Maybe it was them, an' maybe it was somebody else who run the Valley men away from the station."

"Who?" Hamp asked easily.

Bill Buckley looked at him. "Plenty o' borax in the Valley," he stated. "Two companies snakin' it out, an' not enough water holes to go around. Been lookin' for trouble for a long time."

Hamp Cameron leaned against the porch upright and glanced up at the night sky. He'd run across range wars, and wars between cattle and sheep men; he'd seen men kill each other over gold, and over silver and copper ore, but this was new—a war over a substance that could be dug up and processed for one cent a pound!

In all the disputes, Hamp knew, the outfit that won was the outfit with the most guts, the one that hit hardest and most often, and did not pull the punches. Lace Cordell was a man like that, and Stuart Fleming evidently was not. The Valley Borax superintendent had already run for the law.

It meant that Sheila Graham was going to be forced out of business unless Valley Borax had help; someone to stand behind the outfit with big fists and a bigger gun; someone who had nothing to lose and didn't give a damn; someone, for instance, like Cameron, who had never run across a girl like Sheila Graham before, and who was quite sure he never would again if he took the train out of Mormon and Death Valley.

Chapter Six

At nine o'clock the next morning Hamp stepped in the office of Valley Borax Company on the main street. A little bell rang in the rear of the office when he closed the door, and then Sheila Graham appeared, smiling, wearing a white blouse and dark skirt, a white collar with a dark blue ribbon tied in a bow at the front, the color of her eyes.

Hamp stood with his hat in his hands, and he said, "You offered me a job, yesterday, ma'am. It still open?"

He saw the interest come into her eyes as she studied him, and then she said thoughtfully, "You made up your mind pretty quickly."

Hamp shrugged. "Not as hot here as I thought it was," he said blandly. "Figured I'd like to see the Valley after the way you boasted about it."

Sheila Graham smiled openly at him then, and she said, "Will you come to the rear office?"

Hamp followed her around a partition to the small private office in the rear, and he noticed that the back of this building opened on the big Valley Borax yards. Through the window he could see the wagons lined up along the high picket fence. Mules were being led out of a stable at one end of the yard and over to a watering trough. There were more mules in a corral in the center of the yard, and Hamp spotted McCoy out near the corral, talking with Stuart Fleming.

Sheila Graham wrote his name down on a sheet of paper, with his former address as Laramie, Wyoming.

She looked at the name for a moment, and then she said, "Have you had any stage-line experience, or any experience at all in the kind of work we are doing in the Valley?"

Hamp shook his head. "Figured you might need a trouble shooter," he said. "You had a little trouble out at your Devil's Hole station yesterday. Heard the talk in town."

Sheila Graham looked at him closely. "You're a man who likes trouble?" she asked.

Hamp smiled faintly. He looked out the window at Stuart Fleming, and he said, "I don't look for it, ma'am, but I don't run from it, either. There's a time when you have to stop running and face it."

Sheila nodded soberly, a shadow on her face. "We're having our troubles at Valley Borax," she admitted, "and I suppose we can't expect Sheriff Buckley to spend all of his time protecting our property and looking after our interests. You've undoubtedly thought about this job, Mr. Cameron. What did you intend to do?"

"Figured I'd spend a lot of time in the Valley," Hamp told her. "Patrol the road, and be ready to move the minute anything happens. Like to check up on that Devil's Hole raid right away."

He noticed that Fleming was coming toward the office now, and he wondered how the Valley superintendent was going to take this. Shelia Graham was saying, "We'll sign you on, Mr. Cameron, and you can leave for Devil's Hole immediately. There's a rig going out now. You can accompany it."

Hamp nodded and stood up just as Stuart Fleming came through the door from the yard. Fleming looked at Hamp and then at Sheila Graham behind the desk, for one moment surprise in his face, and then he was cool and unperturbed as usual. He said, "How do you do, Cameron?"

"We've just signed on Mr. Cameron as an employee," Sheila told him.

Watching the man closely, Hamp saw his turquoise eyes flick, and then Fleming came toward him, hand outstretched, a broad, warm smile on his smooth-shaven face. "Glad to have you with us, Cameron," Fleming said.

Hamp nodded, but the thought was running through his mind that Fleming didn't like it.

"Mr. Cameron will have a free hand out in the Valley," Sheila was saying. "He intends to prevent, if possible, and investigate any trouble we may have such as the raid on our Devil's Hole station."

Fleming rubbed his jaw thoughtfully. Then he smiled at Hamp and he said, "You're biting off a big piece, Mr. Cameron. I'll co-operate with you, of course, to the best of my ability."

"Obliged," Hamp murmured.

"Mr. Cameron wants to leave for Devil's Hole with the rig going out now," Sheila said.

"Good." Fleming nodded. "Don't know as you'll find anything out there, Cameron. There's not much to go on, according to the men who brought in the report. The two station attendants in charge skipped out; the mules are gone, and the water hole was poisoned. We're sending out two men with fresh mules now."

Hamp took a cigar from his pocket and weighed it in his hand. He said, "Who would want to raid a Valley Borax station, Mr. Fleming?"

Fleming looked at him, and then he shrugged. "Plenty of Piute and Shoshone breeds in the area," he stated, "living in the mountains off the valley. They've stolen mules before."

"And bribed station men to leave?" Hamp smiled. "And poisoned water holes?"

A slight flush came to Fleming's face, but he was still smiling, and his voice was well controlled. He glanced down at Sheila Graham, and then he said, "Do you have any theories, Cameron?"

"Who would stand to profit by a raid on a Valley station?" Hamp asked him. "Who is interested in seeing that Valley Borax goes out of business?"

Stuart Fleming laughed a little. "Naturally, Cordell and Imperial Borax," he stated, "but can I go over there and accuse Cordell of raiding one of our stations? There is no proof at all that he is behind it."

Hamp put the cigar in his mouth, but he didn't light it. He was looking out through the window, watching the men hook teams of mules to the long chain. The big wagons were waiting, water tank hitched on, ready to roll.

"Reckon I wouldn't expect you to see Cordell," Hamp said, "but I'd keep in mind every minute the fact that a Valley Borax loss is an Imperial Borax gain. Cordell knows that, too."

"We're not losing sight of that fact," Fleming said.

"However, I'd be careful not to make accusations that I can't back up."

Hamp smiled at him. "When I make an accusation, mister," he said softly, "I'll be ready to back it up, too."

They went out in the yard after Hamp had shaken hands with Sheila Graham, and she had wished him good luck.

In the yard Fleming introduced Hamp to a number of Valley Borax employees, including the head yard man, Steve Beaumont, a big fellow with a shock of pepper-colored hair and a flattened nose, whom Hamp immediately liked.

Beaumont said, "You're the feller worked on Red Doran of Imperial. Glad to know you, Cameron. Reckon we can use a man with big fists around here."

Little Stub McCoy pumped Hamp's hand vigorously, grinning from ear to ear.

"Anybody figures on buckin' us now," McCoy chuckled, "better think twice. You boys see what he done to that gun sharp last night in the Twenty Mule Saloon?"

Stuart Fleming touched Hamp's arm. He said, "You'll want to pick out a horse, Cameron. Take your choice in the stables."

Hamp nodded and left the crowd of yardmen who had gathered around him. Fleming hadn't said it, and there had been no indication of it in his pleasant face, but Hamp had got the impression that he didn't like this adulation for another man. In this yard Fleming was the big wheel, and he didn't like another man stealing his thunder. Hamp wondered if that was the only reason

Fleming had not been too pleased at his signing on with Valley Borax.

In the stable Hamp picked out a big buckskin, threw a saddle on the animal, and walked him outside. Stub McCoy was waiting for him, sitting astride a little blue roan. He said eagerly:

"What do you figure on doin' at Devil's Hole, Hamp?"

"I'll see when I get there," Hamp murmured.

He watched the driver maneuvering his long string of mules around in the yard, heading them out through the wide entranceway, and then he lifted a hand to Stuart Fleming, who was standing with Steve Beaumont watching, and he rode after the wagons. As he went past the office windows he saw Sheila Graham standing there, looking out, and he touched his hat brim to her. She waved back, smiling at him, and he thought idly that that was another reason for Fleming's displeasure at having him with the company.

The rig rolled up along the main street, Hamp and Stubby McCoy riding with it and the small herd of mules coming along in the rear, two drivers with them.

As they passed Sheriff Buckley's office, Buckley came out to have a look at them, and surprise came into his eyes as he saw Hamp on a Valley Borax horse, riding with the outfit.

Lifting a hand to him, Hamp nodded and smiled, knowing that Buckley would find out very shortly that he had signed up with Valley.

At the next corner Hamp spotted another man, standing under the awning in front of the Piute

64

Saloon—a man in black with a thin face and hooded, colorless eyes.

Merle Wynant looked the other way when Hamp rode past him, and his face was pale and tight.

Stubby McCoy said softly, "Reckon I'd watch that one if I were you, Hamp."

"Aim to," Hamp said.

They passed the last house in town and moved up the slight grade toward Wind Gap, the twenty mules moving at a fairly fast pace, hauling the empty wagons.

Hamp and Stub McCoy rode on ahead now to avoid the dust kicked up by the rig, and they pointed for the break in the ridge where the road dipped down into Death Valley.

A hot breeze hit them as they entered the gap. It was the breath of hell itself coming up out of the Valley, stifling, pregnant with alkali, and Hamp grimaced as he looked at Stubby McCoy.

"We ain't down there yet." McCoy grinned, pointing with his hand.

The Valley came into sight then, and Hamp slowed down to have a good look. It was a dead land, a dry and lifeless land, waves of burning, drying heat coming up from the silvery salt deposits.

Long files of boulders, swept down into the Valley from countless cloudbursts in the mountains on either side, lay scattered across the mouths of canyons. Slate-colored gravel, a half mile wide, alluvial deposits, had been pushed out through canyon mouths across the white expanse.

On all sides were the mountains, dead, void of vegetation, shimmering in the intense heat—the Funerals forming the east wall, the Owlshead on the south, the Last Chance Range on the north, and the Panamint Range to the west.

Stubby McCoy pointed with his finger to a snow-capped mountaintop in the Panamints. He said briefly, "Telescope Peak."

The Valley floor itself was six to fifteen miles wide in places, spotted here and there with mesquite thickets and salt grass. The desert holly that Sheila Graham had mentioned was scattered along the road, very pretty with its silvery leaves and yellowish-green flowers.

Huge ravens fluttered down from the surrounding heights, croaking ominously, the only sound in this dead land, but not the only life. An occasional road runner broke from cover along the graded road and fled on ahead of them, moving with incredible speed, its crested head bobbing.

Stub McCoy said, "How do you like it, Hamp?"

"Hot," Hamp said. "The crows seem to like it."

The road ran as straight as an arrow across a field of broken rock salt, the rock salt lying in chunks two feet high with holes in between them. The road had been literally pounded across this bed, the rock salt beaten down with the sledge hammers, according to Stub McCoy. The hoofs of the mules resounded hollowly on this hard stretch of road.

As they rode along McCoy outlined to Hamp, briefly, the method used by Valley Borax in bringing the product out to civilization.

"Chinamen out at the plant scoop it up," McCoy

explained. "White men can't stand the heat out there. They bring it in on sleds to the reduction plant, where it's boiled down. We see that it gets out to the railhead."

Hamp learned the rest of it as they came off the rock-salt bed. The haul from the plant to Mormon was divided into ten sections, the mules driven sixteen miles per day. Each teamster had one lap of the road and got to know it the way he knew the streets of Mormon. He took a full load out to the next station, returning then with empty wagons. Valley Borax was using ten rigs in the hauls, keeping them moving all the time, maintaining rigid schedules. It was ten days out to the reduction plant and ten days back, a twenty-day schedule.

"Hell on the mules," Stub McCoy stated, "an' hell on the men, but we get it out, an' we aim to keep gettin' it out."

"Have trouble keeping the men in the Valley?" Hamp asked him curiously.

"Have to be relieved pretty often," Stub told him. "Mules don't think an' men do. You stay out here a few weeks an' you got enough. Find yourself talkin' to the pack rats. Time to get out, then, an' hit the high spots in Mormon."

Pulling off the road at noon for the midday meal, and to give the mules a short rest, they watched an Imperial rig roll by, the driver and swamper on the rival wagons staring at them sourly, saying nothing.

"Hell of a bunch," Stub McCoy said as they sat down in the shade of one of the wagons. "That Lace Cordell ain't satisfied makin' eight an' nine cents profit on a cent's worth o' borax. He's after whole hog. Tried to

67

buy out Miss Sheila, but she turned him down."

"Any other outfits in the business?" Hamp asked.

"Was two smaller companies," Stub McCoy told him, "but Cordell bought 'em out, or ran 'em out. Nobody knows which. When he gits Valley he's head man. He'll be able to buy half the state."

"He hasn't got Valley yet," Hamp said.

Stubby McCoy looked at him. "Not yet." He grinned.

They rolled into Devil's Hole station at six in the evening, finding it abandoned, the loaded borax rig standing in the yard adjacent to the stone corral. Hamp had a look at the poisoned water hole, and then Stub McCoy and the swamper with the rig went to work with shovels, digging it out, bailing out the water, until it started to run clear again. The water hole was less than two feet in diameter and two or three feet deep, with the water seeping in from underground springs.

The mules were given water from the water tank and then turned into the corral, the driver and the swamper intending to start the return trip in the morning.

In the rear of the stone hut that served as quarters for the attendants, Hamp washed his face and hands in a bucket of water drawn from the water tank. His face felt gritty, salty, dried out from the long day in the sun, and the water, even though warm, was refreshing.

He sat on a bench in the shade, drying himself, watching Stub McCoy come up with a bucket to go through the same process, and then he said to the little driver, "You know the two attendants Valley Borax had out here?"

Stub nodded contemptuously. "Weren't much good," he stated. "Somebody paid 'em, an' they disappeared."

"With the mules?" Hamp asked.

Stub shook his head. "Don't figure they took the mules," he stated. "Them boys didn't have the nerve to steal animals. They just skipped."

"And the mules are gone," Hamp observed.

Stub McCoy jerked his head toward the east, in the direction of the Funeral Mountains. "Wouldn't be surprised," he said significantly, "if the mules went that way."

"What's up there?" Hamp wanted to know.

"Old Piute City," Stub said, "an' Manuel's Casino. Ain't much o' Piute left—old silver camp—but there's people hangin' around Manuel's place, an' they ain't the best kind o' people. Lot o' breeds, an' the kind o' chaps don't care too much fer the law. Somebody paid 'em, they'd run down here any time to pick up mules an' run 'em back into the mountains where you an' I would never find 'em."

Hamp frowned. "You think that's where our mules went?"

"Eat my hat," Stub McCoy smiled, "if you—don't find mule tracks headin' toward the Funerals. Take a look while I wash this damn face o' mine."

As the little driver plunged his face into the water bucket, Hamp got up, made a short circuit of the stone corral in which the mules had been kept, and easily located the tracks of the missing animals, pointed, as McCoy had predicted, east toward the Funeral Range.

He came back to find McCoy reclining on the bench,

a pipe in his mouth, and he said, "Fleming know about this?"

"Told him when it happened," Stub McCoy said. "Reckon he passed it on to Sheriff Buckley. Bill will take a ride up that way someday, look around Manuel's, find nothin', an' come home again. That ends it. You ain't findin' them mules grazin' in the streets o' Piute City."

"How far is this old silver camp?" Hamp asked him.

"Seven-eight miles back in the mountains," Stub told him. "You go through that gap." He pointed with his pipe. "Find it in the bottom o' the canyon on the other side. Rip-snortin' place ten years ago, but dead now, exceptin' fer Manuel's."

"Who is Manuel?" Hamp wanted to know.

"Mexican chap took over the Casino when the town folded up," Stub McCoy explained. "Don't know much about him. Sells liquor an' supplies to them that wants it an' has the money to pay. Manuel ain't much, but his niece, Rita, kind o' makes up for him."

"Rita?" Hamp murmured.

"See her when you git there," Stub McCoy said calmly. "You leavin' in the mornin'?"

Hamp smiled at him. "How'd you know?" he asked.

Little Stub puffed on his pipe. "I know you, mister," he said softly, "an' damned glad you're on our side."

Chapter Seven

It was well past midnight when Hamp, lying on one of the four bunks in the stone hut, felt a hand on his shoulder, and then heard Stub McCoy's soft voice.

"Company outside," Stub murmured. "You want to have a look?"

Hamp sat up immediately, sliding his feet into his boots and then reaching for his gun belt. As he was strapping it on he said to Stub, "You get a look at them?"

"Dark night," the little driver told him. "Woke up ten minutes ago an' figured I'd have a look around. Too damned hot to sleep, anyway. Spotted these four *hombres* movin' up along the edge o' the mesquite thickets behind the corral. Could be more mule thieves."

Hamp listened to the other two men in the room snoring loudly, and then Stub McCoy whispered, "Reckon I better wake them up, too?"

"Let them sleep," Hamp said softly. "They might get in the way."

"Sure." Stub grinned.

They slipped out through the door, flattening themselves against the wall of the building, and then worked around to the rear in the direction of the corral. The borax rig stood in the yard in front of the corral, looming against the night sky.

Hamp moved around it cautiously, gun in hand, Stub McCoy following him. They could hear the mules moving in the corral restlessly, and then as he crouched near the rear wheel of the water tank, Hamp saw a shadow slipping up along the rock wall of the corral, moving toward the pole gate.

"One of 'em comin'," Stub murmured.

Another figure clambered over the low wall and walked toward the mules, which were bunched over in one corner. Sliding back the hammer of the gun, Hamp stepped from behind the wagon. The man who had been coming toward the gate was less than thirty feet away now, and he kept coming, not seeing Hamp in the shadows.

Hamp said softly, "That's far enough, mister."

Stub McCoy had crawled under the lead wagon, coming out in front of the corral gate. He went up on the wall of the corral, gun in hand, and he called to the man inside, "Throw 'em up, Jack. You're covered."

Hamp was aware of the fact that two of the four men Stub had seen were still unaccounted for, and he watched warily as the man in front of him stopped walking and straightened up, lifting his hands slightly.

"Walk forward," Hamp ordered, "and drop your gun belt."

He noticed that the man inside the corral had stopped, also, and was standing there in the shadows, looking toward Stub McCoy, making no move. Then a gun cracked from the other end of the corral, the bullet splintering one corner of the water tank. The man in front of Hamp suddenly darted toward a clump of mesquite just as a second gun opened up.

Hamp got one shot at him as he dropped to one knee, and then he fired twice at the flashes of the guns at the end of the corral. The man inside the corral had opened fire at Stub McCoy, and when Stub fired back, Hamp saw the raider stagger and go down.

"Got one of 'em!" Stub yelped.

The mules inside the corral had started to circle in fright, kicking up dust. Hamp sprinted toward the mesquite, hearing his man running on ahead of him. He followed, the branches of the mesquite bushes whipping at his face. He could hear the man moving, but was unable to see him until they both came out into a little clearing. He didn't want to shoot now, as he was anxious to take the man prisoner.

They were at the far end of the corral when the raider up ahead stumbled. Sprinting forward, Hamp landed on his back before he could recover himself, and both of them went to the ground.

When Hamp slashed at the man's head with the gun barrel, he felt him go limp. On the other side of the corral he could hear Stub McCoy yelling. There were more shots, and then the sound of a horse plunging away.

Assuming the raiders were making their escape, Hamp rolled his captive over on his back, and then squatted to strike a match. When the match flared up, he looked down into the face of the unconscious man. He didn't recognize the man, but the face made him gasp.

The raider was undoubtedly a breed, dark-skinned, coarse black hair, high cheekbones, the face horribly scarred as if by a mountain lion. The scars were crisscrossed, covering almost every section of the face, running across the nose and the eyes.

He wore a white cotton shirt, and he was hatless. A gun belt was strapped around his waist, however, and he had a knife stuck inside the belt of his pants. When the match flickered out, Hamp crouched to pick the man up and carry him back to the stone hut.

Stub McCoy was calling across the corral, "Hamp—Hamp Cameron!"

Hamp was opening his mouth to answer the call when the sky collapsed on his head. He'd had the scar-faced breed half off the ground, but he let go now, falling across him, and the last thought he had before the darkness closed in on him was that he'd been too hasty with that match, and had attracted one of the other raiders who had not run out.

As he fell forward, something struck him across the head a second time, and he knew no more until he heard Stub McCoy's voice and felt the water on his face.

Stub was saying, "Reckon he's comin' around now. Hand me that whisky."

Hamp felt the fiery liquor sliding down his throat when Stub held the glass to his lips. He opened his eyes then and tried to sit up. He was back inside the stone hut, on his bunk, and Stub was crouching beside him, the two other Valley Borax men looking down at him anxiously.

"How do you feel?" Stub growled.

Hamp shook his head. He felt the back of it gingerly as he sat on the edge of the bunk. It was sore and swollen to the touch.

"Just sit still fer a while," Stub told him. "We ain't goin' no place tonight, anyway."

"They all get away?" Hamp asked him. "The fellow I'd caught, too?"

Stub McCoy looked at him. "Didn't know you'd caught anybody," he said. "Found you on the west side of the corral. Looked like you'd been slugged with a

74

gun barrel. Had a hell of a time findin' you, too."

Hamp grimaced. "I wanted a prisoner," he stated, "somebody to bring back to Mormon. I'd caught this scar-faced breed when somebody came up on me from behind."

"Scar face?" Stub McCoy murmured. "Looked like he'd run into a big cat?"

"Know him?" Hamp asked.

Stub nodded. "Sounds like Piute Charlie. Hangs out in Manuel's Casino." He added thoughtfully, "Only man in these parts with a face like that."

"I'll remember him," Hamp murmured. "What happened to the one you shot in the corral?"

"Dead as a mackerel," Stub told him. "Another breed. Four of 'em must o' come down from Piute City on another raid. Reckon they ain't givin' us much time to git organized around here, Hamp."

"Why did they pick on Devil's Hole station twice in succession?" Hamp asked him.

"Nearest to Piute City," Stub explained. "They kin run down here from the mountains an' head back in no time."

Hamp held a wet towel to the back of his head. "They knew pretty quickly," he said, "that we were bringing fresh mules out here."

"You mean," Stub McCoy said significantly, "that whoever paid 'em knew we was bringin' mules out to Devil's Hole."

"Not too far from Mormon to Piute City, is it?" Hamp asked.

"Seven miles," McCoy said. "So you figure somebody rode out from Mormon to hire these boys to make the raid?"

"How do you figure it?" Hamp asked him.

"Reckon we're thinkin' along the same lines." Stub McCoy smiled coldly. "You aim to find somebody now who'll tell us who paid him to raid a Valley Borax station?"

Hamp nodded. "When we have somebody who will talk, we turn him over to Buckley."

"Reckon you got to have proof with Bill Buckley," Stub said. "When Bill sticks his neck out he's got to know he's right."

"He'll know," Hamp promised.

"Maybe I better go along to Piute City," Stub said.

"They know you over there?" Hamp asked him.

Stub nodded and frowned. "Been around this way a long time," he said. "Reckon they'd know me."

"I'd better go alone," Hamp told him.

"You better walk careful," Stub McCoy warned. "That's a tough crowd in Manuel's Casino."

They went back to bed, this time leaving one of the crew on guard at the corral. Hamp's head still ached, and it was some time before he was able to sleep.

When he awoke, a little after dawn, Stub already had the coffee boiling and bacon sizzling in the pan. "Rise an' shine," Stub said.

A Valley borax rig rolled in as they were eating, and Stub made arrangements to accompany it back to Mormon while Hamp rode over to Piute City.

"I'll tell Fleming what happened last night," Stub said. "Reckon he'll have to send more men out to each

76

station now if we got to fight off raids on our mules."

Hamp finished the last of his coffee, looked into the cup, and said, "You won't have to tell Fleming where I'm going."

Stub McCoy looked at him curiously. "No?"

Hamp shook his head. "He'll find out when I come back."

"He'll ask," Stub persisted.

Hamp smiled. "Tell him I'm chasing stray mules," he said.

"Sure," Stub murmured, but Hamp could see that he was still a little puzzled.

At seven in the morning Hamp saddled the buckskin, nodded to Stub, who was watching him from the seat of the lead borax wagon, and then rode east toward the Funeral Range and the gap that led to Piute City.

Stub waved a hand to him and called a last warning to be careful. Moving around the stone corral, Hamp heard the big wagons rolling, the driver cracking his whip, yelling.

Beyond the corral, he picked up the trail of the raiders who had struck at them the previous night. The tracks led due east toward the gap in the mountains.

He rolled a cigarette as he let the buckskin pick its own way along. There was no rush now, because the raiders would probably go no farther than Piute City, and he knew one of them. The difficulty now lay in locating the man and getting him out of the old mining camp back to Mormon and Sheriff Buckley. If Piute Charlie could be made to talk, they had Lace Cordell over a barrel.

The sun hit him full in the face as he rode toward the purple mountain range, and then as the sun rose higher, the color of the mountains changed. They looked unreal, like painted ridges against the brassy sky, shimmering in the heat. The purple gave way to brown, splashed with the darker shadows of the canyons. A buzzard sailed out of a nearby canyon, and Hamp rode into the canyon, grateful for the shade afforded by one wall.

The trail of the three raiders led up into the mountains, twisting around huge boulders strewn along canyon floors. Constantly he lost the tracks on rocky ground, and, not particularly caring, picked them up again as he followed the easiest route toward the gap.

At noon he camped at the base of a high cliff, watering the buckskin from the big water bag he had slung over the saddle. He had a meal of cold beans and bacon, washed down with water from the bag, and then he rode into the gap, spotting the old mining camp a half hour later as he was emerging on the other side.

Piute City lay in a notch of the mountains, some of the buildings clinging to the north wall of the notch. Mountain piñon grew here on the west wall of the range, and up above the tops of the trees Hamp saw the rusted smokestacks of the abandoned stamp mills, and the sprawling buildings of the mills themselves.

It was a dead town with smoke lifting into the air from only a few of the buildings. There seemed to be three streets running parallel to each other, the main street at the bottom of the notch and two smaller streets north of the main street. Even from that distance he could see that quite a few of the buildings had already caved in.

He sat there for some time, looking at the town, and then he let the buckskin pick its way down the notch and on to the main street. It was nearly three o'clock in the afternoon when he entered the town, a dry, dusty town with the weeds cropping up along the main street, the hitch racks empty, and most of the buildings boarded up.

From one of the false-front buildings, out of which smoke was emerging, a man came out to have a look at Hamp as he rode by. Hamp lifted a hand to him and kept going in the direction of the largest building in town, at the far end of the street.

It was a two-story building with a porch encircling the entire front. Across the front of it in huge gilt letters, the paint peeling from them, was the word "Casino."

There were wagon sheds and stables to the rear of the structures, and Hamp spotted a few horses under the shed to the right of the building. A man sat on the porch, rocking gently in an old rocker, a cigar in his mouth, and as Hamp drew closer he recognized the man and stared at him curiously.

The man with the cigar in his mouth was Sheriff Bill Buckley of Mormon. Buckley lifted a hand, took the cigar from his mouth, and said, "Reckon you better put that animal under the shed where there's a little shade."

Hamp had slowed down as he came up to the porch. He nodded now and walked the horse around the building to the nearest shed, dismounting and then looking for a water trough. He found one over near the stable and he watered the buckskin again before tying the animal under the shed.

When he came back to the porch he found Bill Buckley in the same position, boots on the rail, the cigar tilted toward the porch ceiling, staring down the street, no expression on his face. He lifted a finger to Hamp and grinned, nodding toward another chair.

"You get around," Hamp told him. He caught the cigar Buckley tossed to him and put it in his mouth.

"My job," Bill Buckley observed, "is to get around, mister. Fleming tells me he's lost mules out at Devil's Hole. Figured I'd have a look around here. Most trouble in the Valley starts in Piute City, in Manuel's Casino."

Hamp eased himself into the chair. He watched a Mexican swamper come out through the swinging doors with a pail of slop and toss it over the railing into the street, and then he said, "After mules myself, Sheriff."

Bill Buckley nodded. "Figured you'd be along here," he said calmly. "Fleming told me you were signed up with Valley Borax an' headed out into Death Valley. Didn't think you'd find anything out at Devil's Hole, which meant you'd be comin' up this way for a look."

"Found more than I thought I'd find," Hamp murmured, and he saw Buckley glance at him quickly.

"How's that?" Buckley asked.

"Another raid on Valley mules last night," Hamp told him. "We shot one of them. Three others got away, but I got a good look at one—a breed. Stub says he goes by the name of Piute Charlie."

80

"Piute Charlie," Bill Buckley said softly. "Reckon he'll be in this way after dark. Lives out in the hills somewhere."

The Sheriff of Mormon got up from the chair and nodded toward the bat-wing doors. They went into the saloon to find it empty, save for an enormous fat man with an oily face, half asleep at the far end of the bar, a dirty bartender's apron around his waist, his shirt open at the neck, revealing a mass of black hair on his chest.

The main saloon and gambling room was very large, but only a portion of it seemed to be in use. Many of the tables and chairs were stacked in a corner of the room, gathering dust. On the shelves behind the bar were liquor bottles, but only a few of the shelves were filled.

Bill Buckley said sharply, "Manuel."

The fat bartender awoke with a start and waddled toward them, smiling. He had black, snakelike eyes, very much alive now, darting from Hamp to Buckley and then back to Hamp again.

Buckley said, "Piute Charlie been around, Manuel?"

The fat man broke out into a torrent of Spanish. Hamp listened uncomprehendingly. When Buckley looked at him he shrugged his shoulders, and Buckley said simply, "He says Charlie hasn't been around in three days an' owes him for plenty o' drinks."

Hamp nodded and put both elbows on the bar. When he turned his head slightly he saw a girl watching him from a doorway that led to the rear rooms. She was fairly tall with a full figure and jet-black hair. Her dark eyes were fixed on Hamp curiously, recognizing him as a stranger in this place.

Looking at her, Hamp felt his heart begin to beat a little faster. She was quite a beautiful girl, with full, curved lips and dark lashes. There was a faint smile playing around the corners of her perfect mouth.

Bill Buckley ordered drinks, and then as he turned he spotted the girl in the doorway. He touched his hat, smiled, but didn't say anything. The girl came out through the doorway, went past them and out onto the porch.

Hamp put his glass down and said, "That would be Rita."

Bill Buckley smiled a little. "You keep your ears open, Cameron," he observed. "That's Rita Sánchez, Manuel's niece, and well able to take care of herself even in a place like this."

"She could be in a better place," Hamp told him. He heard the bat-wing doors swinging behind him, but he didn't turn to look. He expected to be around here some time, waiting for Piute Charlie to turn up, and there would be ample opportunities to meet Rita Sánchez if he wanted to meet her.

Bill Buckley waited until fat Manuel had ambled back to the fly-specked newspaper he'd been sleeping over when they came in, and then he said, "You'll wait here for Charlie to come in?"

Hamp nodded. "He doesn't know me, and I know him, but I'll still keep out of sight. When we catch him I intend to find out who sent him over to Devil's Hole to steal mules."

Buckley toyed with the glass. "Some of these breeds," he said idly, "don't need anybody to send 'em,

Cameron. They just steal for the hell of it. Been stealin' all their lives."

"This bunch was sent," Hamp said.

Buckley rubbed his chin. "You mean Cordell?" he asked.

"Who else," Hamp asked him, "wants to see Valley Borax forced out of business?"

Sheriff Buckley pushed his glass away and looked at Hamp in the cracked bar mirror. "If it's Cordell," he said quietly, "he'll have to talk to me, but you'll have to prove it's Cordell."

"Will you believe Piute Charlie?" Hamp wanted to know.

Buckley smiled a little. "Reckon I'd like to hear his story before I believe anything," he said.

Hamp nodded. "That's good enough for me," he said, and then he strolled toward the bat-wing doors and stood there, looking over them. He saw Rita Sánchez standing at the far end of the porch, her back toward him, looking toward the distant mountains, and then as he watched her she turned as if expecting him to be there, and she smiled at him. She wore a white blouse and a dark, flower-embroidered skirt.

Touching his hat brim to her, Hamp went back to the bar. Bill Buckley said to him over his shoulder, "When you're chasing a man, Cameron, never let a woman come in between you. You didn't the last time."

"The last time," Hamp Cameron said softly, "was different, Sheriff."

Chapter Eight

At five in the afternoon Bill Buckley rode off, leaving Hamp sitting on the porch of the Casino.

"If Piute Charlie spots me in town," Buckley explained, "he'll never come near it. I'll be close by, Cameron."

Hamp nodded and lifted a hand to him as he rode off. He sat on the porch smoking a cigar, looking down the weed-grown street. An old prospector came in from the hills, plodding along behind three burros, dusty, dried out, his clothes hanging from his lean frame like the clothes of a scarecrow.

As the old man sat down on the top step of the porch, Hamp said to him, "Luck?"

The old prospector stared at him, his eyes red-rimmed from the heat and the dust out of which he had come.

"It's out there, mister," he said. "I ain't found it, but it's out there." He nodded toward the purple ridges, and the valley of hell beyond.

"You ever get tired looking for it?" Hamp asked.

The old man smiled wanly. "Never git tired lookin'," he stated sagely. "It's when you stop, mister, is when you git tired."

Hamp nodded. "Step inside," he invited. "Have a drink on me. Tell Manuel I'll stand it."

The old man went inside and came out a few minutes later wiping his mouth with the back of his coat sleeve. "Obliged," he said.

"You know Piute Charlie?" Hamp asked him.

The prospector nodded. "Know him, but ain't seen him in a month, mister. I'm in here an' I'm out o' here."

Hamp nodded. He said no more, and the old man eventually moved around to the rear sheds to look after his burros. When he was gone the bat-wing doors squeaked gently again, and without looking around, Hamp Cameron knew who was coming out. The Casino had been empty save for Manuel, who probably never had gone beyond the confines of his bar.

A skirt swished behind him, and then he heard a soft, musical voice.

Rita Sánchez said, "It is a good man who will buy an old man a drink."

She spoke English perfectly, and Hamp glanced up at her in surprise, not having expected this after hearing Manuel, her uncle. He watched the Mexican girl come over and sit on the porch rail in front of him, and then he said casually, "Sometimes a drink pays for itself, señorita."

Her hair was blue-black, and she wore a yellow flower in it. There was no Indian blood in her. He was quite sure of that. Her nose was perfectly formed, unlike the stubby, flattened noses of the local Piutes and Shoshones. Her eyes were dark, but not with the oily blackness of the Indian. She said, "Who are you looking for, señor?"

Hamp smiled and looked at the cigar in his hand. "Reckon I didn't say I was looking for anyone, ma'am."

Rita shrugged. "In this place," she smiled, "a man comes either looking or running away. You do not act like a man who is running away."

"Could be," Hamp observed, "I'm just passing through."

"A man passing through," Rita said, "is not acquainted with Sheriff Buckley of Mormon." She added thoughtfully, "And you are not passing through, señor. You are waiting."

Hamp flipped the cigar butt over the porch railing. "A waiting man," he said, "is sometimes a hungry man. Can I get a meal here, Señorita Sánchez?"

"That can be arranged," Rita Sánchez said. "Will you come with me to the kitchen?"

Hamp stood up. He followed her inside, past the still dozing Manuel at the bar, and then through a side door into the big kitchen. A coffeepot was boiling on the stove, along with a pot of beans. A number of tortillas lay on a sideboard, ready to be fried, and Hamp, seeing them, looked at the girl quickly.

"You expected company?" he asked.

"You," she said simply. "You have been sitting on the porch for some time. You came in without a pack horse and you do not have supplies. I assumed you would be wanting to eat shortly."

Hamp smiled. He sat down at the little table along the wall, and he sat facing the door from the bar, watching the girl as she set before him a plate and a coffee cup.

She paused in front of him after she had put the coffee cup down, and she said, "I might be able to help you find the man you are looking for, señor."

Hamp nodded. "You might," he admitted, "and then again you might be able to warn him off. *Quien sabe?*"

Rita Sánchez stood there, smiling at him, finding

86

some humor in the situation, and looking at her, Hamp Cameron remembered that for nearly two years he had given no thought to women as he had pursued a man. Two years was a long time, and the girl in front of him was very beautiful and very desirable. They were alone in this part of the building, and outside slept a fat man, who seemingly had little interest in what his niece did.

Hamp put his hand out and placed it on her arm, and then he stood up. He said softly, "Who said I was looking for a *man,* señorita?"

She did not draw away, and she continued to smile at him, small pin points of light dancing in her eyes.

He said, "You are a very beautiful woman, Miss Sánchez."

"Other men have told me that," Rita Sánchez said casually.

Hamp smiled. "Are there *men* around here?" he asked.

"There have been."

Hamp looked down at her, and then for the first time since coming to this place he thought of Sheila Graham. He had remained in Mormon because he had become interested in Sheila, and now while working for her, drawing pay from her company, he was suddenly absorbed in a girl who was admitting to him that other men came to see her. Buckley knew her, and had warned him to be careful. Other men in Mormon knew her, possibly men like Lace Cordell and Red Doran, his driver.

He had been holding both her arms, and he dropped his hands now and sat down again, frowning.

Rita Sánchez laughed softly. "You have another girl," she said complacently, and she walked back to the stove.

"No," Hamp told her, but the color came to his face.

"I know," Rita said from the stove.

Hamp listened to the tortillas frying, and he stared at the coffee cup in front of him. When Rita Sánchez came back from the stove he said to her quietly, "Reckon I owe you an apology, señorita."

"You did no wrong." The Mexican girl smiled. "You are a good man, and I must give you some advice. This is not a good place for a good man. If you have no business here, you had better ride out."

"I have business," Hamp told her. "I'll wait."

As he was eating he heard men coming in to the barroom outside. It was growing dark in the hills, and the owls were slipping out of the shadows, heading for this dim, tawdry light of Manuel's Casino. These were the men who lived in the darkness, whom the law sought in vain. Barred from honest communities, they sought refuge here in the hills, and they came to Manuel's each night to solace themselves with Manuel's cheap liquor, and perhaps, but Hamp Cameron did not think so, with Manuel's pretty niece.

Finishing his second cup of coffee, Hamp stood up. He put a bill down on the table and said, "I'll use the back door if you don't mind."

"Be careful," Rita warned him again.

Hamp smiled at her. "I don't aim to die," he told her, and then he went out the back door and into the yard in front of the stables. He had a look at the buckskin under the shed, walked around until he located a Mexican boy, who evidently served as hostler here, and had him bring oats and water to the horse.

Then he walked around to the front porch of the Casino and went up the steps and into the saloon. The first man he saw at the bar, half facing him, a glass of liquor in his hand, was the breed Piute Charlie, his scarred face hideous in the dim yellow light of the overhead lamps.

There were a half-dozen other men at the bar, and Hamp was positive some of them had been with Piute Charlie on the raid at Devil's Hole. Most of them had the flattened faces and dark Indian eyes of half-breeds, although they wore white men's clothing.

Every man at the bar turned to look when Hamp came in and took a position at the bar a half-dozen feet from where Piute Charlie stood. They didn't know him. He had been positive they wouldn't, because when he'd been struck from behind at the Devil's Hole corral, it had been very dark, and they had undoubtedly left in haste.

Rita, who evidently waited behind the bar with her uncle, came toward him, nodding impersonally. Hamp pointed to a bottle on the shelf, and she took it down, sliding bottle and glass toward him. When he looked at her, he saw the warning look in her eyes.

There was no talk in the barroom, although some of the men had been talking when Hamp came in. He was the stranger here, and therefore the damper on the conversation. Until they knew him, they had to remain silent. Only the pursued and the pursuers came to

Manuel's Casino, and they had not yet labeled him.

Taking the bottle and the glass to a corner table, Hamp sat down, facing the bar. He poured his drink, and then he picked up a deck of greasy cards, shuffled them, and arranged them on the wood in front of him for a game of solitaire.

After a while the men at the bar relaxed a little. They were still suspicious of him, but they felt no personal fear of him. If he had been a law hound after one of them, he would have made his play before this.

Hamp dealt himself cards, studied them, and laid them out in the formation, watching Piute Charlie at the bar, watching the other men in the room, and watching the door. Piute Charlie was the man he wanted, and the man he had to bring back to Mormon, but walking up to him and taking him prisoner was not that simple. Very possibly some of the men in the room were Charlie's friends or relatives, and they could conceivably take a hand in the affair, making it very difficult.

There was, also, the matter of Bill Buckley. The Sheriff of Mormon had promised to be close by, to aid in the capture of Charlie, but as yet Buckley had not made his appearance.

Hamp smoked his cigar and sipped his drink and played his hand and waited, knowing that he had to keep Charlie in sight, no matter where he went or what he did.

Then the bat-wing doors opened, and Hamp, thinking it was Buckley coming on the scene, pushed his chair back slightly and put both hands on the table, ready to get up quickly.

90

The man coming into the room was the cold-eyed killer Merle Wynant, Lace Cordell's hired hand. Wynant spotted him immediately at the corner table, and hatred came into his pale eyes. He looked at Hamp and looked away, and then stepped up to the bar.

Hamp watched for some sign of recognition between Wynant and Piute Charlie, but there was none. He was quite sure, though, that Wynant, the Imperial Borax hand, had arranged that raid on the Valley Borax station the previous night, using disreputable characters like Piute Charlie to do the actual dirty work.

Piute Charlie looked in Wynant's direction, once, and then nursed his drink, smoking at the same time a Mexican cigarillo. The breed watched every move Rita Sánchez made behind the bar, and Hamp was quite sure he'd be staying close by the Casino the remainder of the evening. The strategy, then, was to wait for the arrival of Sheriff Buckley and close in on Piute Charlie, defying the others in the room to make a play if they chose to.

An hour passed, and Buckley still did not arrive. Restlessly, Hamp threw away the cards, paid for his drink at the bar, leaving the bottle there, and went out on the porch. A card game had started up in one corner of the room, and Wynant was in it. Piute Charlie had been talking with another breed at the far end of the bar, and he was sitting down now, still with the same man.

Standing on the porch, Hamp looked up the desolate main street. A few spots of light showed in the line of darkened buildings. To the rear of the Casino, in the sheds and stable, horses stamped restlessly.

There were four animals tied to the hitch rack directly in front of the saloon, and as Hamp watched them, the doors opened behind him and Wynant came out. The little gunman stood out near the top step of the walk, less than six feet from where Hamp stood, one shoulder against the porch pillar, his coat open and his gun in sight.

Wynant said softly, his voice almost shaking with intensity, "I haven't forgotten you, mister."

Hamp looked at him. "That right?" he murmured.

"I'll pay you back," Wynant told him.

"When?" Hamp asked him. "Now?"

"Never mind," Wynant snarled.

Hamp turned to face him, putting the small of his back against the pillar now, and he said slowly, his voice very cold, "If you shoot at me from an alley, Wynant, you'd better not miss."

"Why not?" the gun sharp asked.

"Because I'm coming after you," Hamp told him. "I followed one man for two years. I'll follow you for twenty, if I have to, and I'll catch up with you. Somewhere, someday, I'll catch up with you. You'll never shoot again from an alley."

Wynant laughed, a grim, disdainful laugh, and then he went down the steps, mounted a sorrel horse carrying the brand of the Emerald Livery, in town, and rode away in the direction of Mormon.

Hamp watched him go, and then he turned his head to look in over the bat-wing doors. Piute Charlie was still talking with the second breed, sitting with his back against the side wall, but Rita Sánchez had come out from behind the bar and was walking toward the doors. She came out into the patch of yellow light on the porch, walked out into the shadows where Hamp stood, and said, "You haven't found him, señor?"

Hamp shrugged. "Waiting," he said.

"Dead men wait, too," Rita told him. "Don't be a fool. If you have business, attend to it, and go away."

"You are concerned about me?" Hamp asked her curiously.

He looked at her face in the dim light, and he heard her say simply, "When a man puts his hand on me and then steps away, I am concerned about that man."

"I'm obliged," Hamp murmured.

"Is she worthy of you?" Rita Sánchez asked softly.

Hamp pursed his lips. "I didn't mention a woman," he said.

The Mexican girl sighed. "She is a very fortunate girl," she said. "Now what can I do for you, señor?"

Hamp frowned a little. He was becoming restless now, thinking of Bill Buckley. Possibly Buckley was chasing a false trail somewhere, and would not be getting back to Piute City tonight. In a few minutes Piute Charlie might suddenly get up and leave with some of his friends, which would complicate matters.

If he could get Charlie out here, alone, he was positive he could handle the man. A gun barrel across Piute Charlie's skull back near the sheds would silence him. He could temporarily borrow one of the old prospector's donkeys, tie and gag the breed, and ride him the seven miles to Mormon this very night, putting him safely in Bill Buckley's jailhouse in town.

Hamp said casually, "You know Piute Charlie inside?"

Rita Sánchez frowned. "He's a bad one," she said.

"Tell him," Hamp said, "that a friend of his is waiting to see him back by the sheds."

"I will tell him you are that friend?" Rita asked, puzzled.

Hamp shook his head. "Tell him the short man in black with the thin face, who just left here, wants to talk with him."

Rita Sánchez hesitated. "You will leave, then?" she asked.

"With Piute Charlie."

"Then you are a law man," Rita murmured. "You are working with Sheriff Buckley?"

Hamp shrugged. "Tonight, yes," he admitted.

He saw her shake her head as if in exasperation. "Piute Charlie has many friends and relatives in these hills," she warned him. "You will be careful?"

Hamp thought about that. "What about you?" he asked suddenly. "Will I be getting you in trouble here?"

Rita Sánchez smiled faintly in the darkness. "I, too, have many friends," she stated, "more than Piute Charlie. I am not afraid."

Hamp reached out and touched her hand. "I am glad," he said, "that I am one of your friends."

Rita Sánchez said nothing. She turned and walked back into the saloon. Hamp went down the steps and moved quickly over toward the sheds. He stood just inside, hidden from sight, but able to watch the porch.

He was not sure yet that Piute Charlie would step into

the trap, but he was quite sure that Wynant was the man who had hired Charlie and the others, and that he had come down tonight to pay them off. Seeing a Valley Borax man in town, he'd decided to wait until another time.

On the other hand, if Charlie knew that Wynant was outside, asking for him, he would surely come, looking for his money, suspecting nothing.

A minute passed, and then another, and Hamp was quite sure Charlie had become suspicious and slipped out the back door. Then the doors opened and the breed came out, alone.

Hamp smiled in satisfaction. Rita Sánchez must have waited deliberately, giving him plenty of time to make his preparations at the shed.

Piute Charlie was short and chunky, and he wore a dun-colored, peaked hat. As he came out through the doors, Hamp had a good look at his scarred face. He slipped the Smith and Wesson .44 from the holster, took a firm grip on the butt, and waited.

Piute Charlie walked out to the edge of the porch, stopped there for one moment, and then died. The gun banged from the opposite side of the street, from an alley between two tumble-down buildings.

The breed clutched at his stomach, bent over double, and then pitched forward, his head striking the wooden step with a sickening thud. He rolled, and then lay still on the walk below.

Hamp broke from the shed, gun in hand, racing toward the alley. As he came up to it, he heard a horse running away in the night. Men were coming out of the

Casino now, and Hamp, knowing that it was useless to give chase to the man who had been in the alley, crossed the road, his gun still in his hand.

He saw Rita Sánchez come out and stand on the porch above them, tall and stately, very stiff. When she saw him coming into the light he noticed that she relaxed.

A man who had been bending over Piute Charlie straightened up and said, "Dead as hell. Never even drew his gun."

He was not one of the breeds in the place, but a hard-case who had been at the card table. He looked at Hamp accusingly, and Hamp handed him his gun, the others staring at him grimly.

"That gun been used?" Hamp asked him.

The barrel was cold. When the gun was broken, the hard case held it up to the light for all to see. None of the cartridges had been used.

"Shot came from the alley across the road," Hamp said simply. "I went over there."

He could hear a horse pounding down the street, now, coming toward them at a fast gallop. When the rider stepped from the saddle. Hamp recognized him as Bill Buckley.

The concern showed in Buckley's gaunt face as he came into the light, and he said brusquely, "All right, all right. What is it?" Then he saw Hamp and he took a deep breath.

A man in the crowd said, "Reckon Piute Charlie got it, Sheriff. Somebody shot him full o' holes."

Bill Buckley went over to look at the dead man, and then he straightened up. Hamp moved back into the shadows as two men picked up Piute Charlie's body and carried it around to the sheds. Sheriff Buckley came over to where Hamp was standing, and said quietly:

"What happened? I heard the shot an' I thought it was you. I came up as fast as I could."

Hamp told him briefly of his plan to get the breed out of the Casino, and of the shot from the alley.

"Waited for you," Hamp said, "but I figured you'd be on another trail, and I didn't want Charlie to run out on us."

Bill Buckley nodded. "Reckon it was my fault," he said morosely. "I located Piute Charlie's shack out in the hills, an' I waited there, hopin' he'd turn up. Then I headed for Piute City an' I heard that shot as I was comin' into town."

"You didn't hear a rider going the other way?" Hamp asked him. "Back off the main street?"

Sheriff Buckley shook his head. "Came on pretty fast," he stated. "Who do you figure was hidin' back in that alley?"

Hamp laughed coldly. "Somebody who didn't want Piute Charlie to be taken back to Mormon, where he would talk," he said. "Wynant, Lace Cordell's man, had been in the Casino a few minutes before. He rode off toward Mormon, but he very easily could have circled and come back to the alley to have his shot at Charlie. He may have suspected I was there to get the breed, and he put him out of the way."

Buckley said with some exasperation, "We still don't have anything on Cordell, an' now with Piute Charlie dead we have to start all over again. All my fault,

Cameron. Had no damn business waitin' that long at Charlie's place. Should o' known he'd be comin' this way long before this."

"I could have waited longer, too," Hamp told him. "I brought Charlie out and played right into Wynant's hands."

"You figure it was Wynant?" Buckley asked slowly. Hamp looked at him in the darkness. "Who else?" he said.

Buckley shook his head. "Can't prove a damn thing," he growled, "an' a law man needs proof."

"We'll get the proof," Hamp told him. "Cordell is bound to overstep himself, and we'll have him."

"I'll watch that Wynant," Buckley promised. "I'll dog him everywhere he goes."

Hamp was looking past him, toward the porch of the Casino, where Rita Sánchez stood, looking in their direction. He had a friend here—a girl who liked and respected him. He wondered if he were a fool riding away from something like this.

Chapter Nine

At nine o'clock the next morning Hamp came out of the lunchroom adjoining the Paradise Hotel, walked the one block to the Valley Borax office, and stepped inside.

He found Sheila Graham and Stuart Fleming in the rear office, and Sheila's face lighted up when she saw him.

"Worried about you," she said as she held out her

hand to him. "Stub told us you'd gone into Piute City after the raiders."

Hamp took her hand, and it was warm and friendly. He glanced at Stuart Fleming, who was standing by the door, a cigar in his mouth, ready to go out into the yard. Fleming's wavy, corn-silk hair was neatly combed; he was clean-shaven, cool even in the early heat of this morning. He wore a clean white shirt and a black string tie.

"Rode in late last night with Sheriff Buckley," Hamp explained.

"You pick up Piute Charlie?" Fleming asked him.

Hamp shook his head. "Shot before we could get to him," he said. "Somebody beat us to it."

Fleming frowned. "Then you learned nothing," he said.

Hamp looked at him. He said evenly, "We learned that whoever is raiding Valley Borax is ready to kill now. Reckon that's something, Mr. Fleming."

Sheila Graham's violet eyes were worried. "What does Sheriff Buckley think about this?" she asked. "You say he was with you in Piute City?"

Hamp nodded. "Met him there. He was trying to check on those raiders, also. Buckley can't do a thing until he has proof that Cordell is hitting at our stations."

"Any way we can get proof?" Fleming asked him.

"We almost had it last night." Hamp scowled. "We were a few minutes away from it. I'm sure Piute Charlie would have talked if we'd got him back to Mormon."

"What happens now?" Fleming wanted to know.

99

"We keep trying," Hamp told him. "I'd suggest you put extra guards out at each station; put a guard with your wagons on the road."

Stuart Fleming frowned and glanced at Sheila Graham. Then he said to Hamp, "I'm afraid that, financially, we're unable to do that, Cameron. Valley Borax would have to take on a lot of extra hands, and we'd be hard-pressed financially."

Hamp looked at Sheila, and she nodded soberly. "My father rather extended himself just before he died," she explained. "He had a number of new wagons built, and we bought a hundred mules to stock the stations. I'm still paying off that debt."

"And the chances are Cordell knows that," Hamp said. "If he can just keep pecking away at Valley Borax, weakening it by these raids, you'll be unable to operate. Is that right, Miss Graham?"

"We'd have to close down," Sheila admitted. "If we can't get the borax to the railhead there are no profits, and the maintenance, salaries, and cost of hay and feed are just as high. In a very short while we'd be in serious difficulty if the wagons stopped coming in."

"I'll see what I can do," Fleming promised, "using some of the yard men as extra guards with the rigs. It's the best we can do for the present."

Hamp saw Stubby McCoy hurrying toward them across the yard, and he sensed immediately that Stub was bringing bad news. The little driver's face was grim as he entered, and he said to Fleming succinctly, "Number Four rig raided four miles east o' Prospector's Hill. Masked riders. Chased our boys off, took the mules, an' burned the wagons. Ben just came in with the news."

Sheila Graham turned away without a word to look out the window.

Stuart Fleming said bitterly, "Twenty more valuable mules gone and two expensive wagons burned. We've got to stop this, Cameron!"

Hamp said to Stub McCoy, "Masked riders?"

"Half dozen of 'em," McCoy said. "Our two boys with the rig didn't have a chance. They made a run fer it to the next station, an' this masked bunch didn't go after 'em."

Stuart Fleming said, "When did this happen, Stub?"

"Four o'clock this mornin'," McCoy told him. "Number Four was makin' a night run, comin' in toward Salt Creek Station."

Sheila Graham turned around. Her voice was unsteady as she spoke. She said, "What are we going to do, Stuart?"

Hamp stood there, his hat in his hand, noticing how she had turned to Fleming in this hour of trouble, and remembering that the last time Fleming had passed the buck to Sheriff Buckley, taking no action himself. It was Sheila herself who had hired a trouble shooter. He had his moment of jealousy here, knowing that it was foolish. Fleming and Sheila Graham had been close associates for some time now, running Valley Borax. It was to be expected that she'd turn to him, and not to a man who but a few days before had been a total stranger.

"I'll see Sheriff Buckley," Fleming said. "We'll take a

ride out into the Valley. We might be able to pick up tracks."

"Pick up tracks," Stub McCoy told him, "but you won't foller 'em far, Mr. Fleming. When they head up into the mountains you lose 'em. They circle an' they go back to Piute City or Mormon, or wherever in hell they come from."

Fleming frowned and looked at Hamp. "What would you suggest, Cameron?" he asked.

"Figured I'd look up Lace Cordell," Hamp told him, and he saw Sheila Graham turn and look at him quickly.

"Will that do any good?" she asked.

"I'll find out." Hamp smiled thinly.

"You can't walk up and accuse him of raiding our outfits," Fleming observed. "We have no proof at all."

"We know damn well he's doin' it, though," Stub McCoy growled.

The doorbell jangled behind them, and they saw Sheriff Buckley coming in, concern on his gaunt, plain face. He said to Sheila quietly, "Heard you had another raid on your outfit, Miss Graham. Ben Rollins told me."

"Third attempt in a week," Stuart Fleming growled. Just coming over to see you, Bill."

Buckley looked at Hamp. "What do you think?" he asked.

Hamp shrugged. "It wasn't Piute Charlie this time," he stated, "but it could have been a crowd from Piute City somebody hired for the occasion."

He put on his hat and he turned to go, and then Bill Buckley put a hand on his arm. The Sheriff of Mormon said, "Been thinkin' on the way over here how we might grab this bunch."

"How's that?" Hamp asked him.

Buckley turned to Fleming. "You got an empty rig leavin' Mormon today?"

Fleming nodded. "Number Six rig pulls out a little after noon, an empty moving out to the processing plant. Stub, here, will handle that outfit to Devil's Hole Station."

Bill Buckley nodded. "If this bunch is raidin' Valley Borax wagons, the chances are they'll hit at this empty, too. They've been doin' most o' the raidin' close by Piute City. This last one wasn't more than eight-nine miles from Piute."

"I've thought of that," Fleming told him. "I'll send two yard men along with the outfit, or even more if you think it wise."

Buckley shook his head. "Scare 'em off," he stated. "They'll let this rig go through an' hit the next one."

"Makes sense," Stub McCoy agreed.

"Thing to do," Buckley went on, "is not let 'em know you got boys ridin' with the outfit. Put 'em inside where they won't be seen, an' then when the raiders arrive, give 'em hell."

Hamp looked into the man's steady brown eyes and his gaunt homely face, and he said, "Reckon you've got something there, Sheriff. I'd like to be in that wagon when it rolls out."

"Might catch some big fish," Bill Buckley told him. "Worth tryin', anyway."

He looked at Stuart Fleming, and the Valley Borax superintendent nodded.

"We'll fix up one of the wagons," he said. "I'll arrange for at least a half-dozen extra men to accompany the outfit."

Sheila Graham spoke up from the window where she was standing. She said to Bill Buckley, "Mr. Cameron intends to speak to Mr. Cordell concerning these raids."

Buckley turned to Hamp and frowned at him. "What in hell will that get you?" he asked.

Hamp shrugged. "Reckon I'll feel a little better," he said.

Buckley pointed a finger at him. "In this town," he warned, "I represent the law, Cameron. I'll arrest the first man who pulls a gun."

Hamp smiled coldly. "You might have to bury the first man to pull a gun, Sheriff," he said, and he walked out through the door.

It was another hot, brassy day with the dogs already beginning to pant at this hour of the morning. Hamp walked down the shady side of the street, passing the front of the hotel, and then crossing in the direction of the Imperial Borax office.

As he came up on the walk he saw Merle Wynant, the gun thrower, watching him over the bat-wing doors of the Piute Saloon, adjacent to the Imperial office.

Stepping into the Imperial office, Hamp saw a thin, bespectacled, hawk-nosed clerk get up from a chair on the other side of a board partition. He said to the clerk, "Cordell in?"

The hawk-nosed man jerked his head in the direction of the Piute Saloon. "Having a drink with a customer," he stated. "Come around later, mister."

Hamp smiled at him. "I'm here now," he said, and he turned and went outside. Wynant was still standing behind the bat-wing doors, watching, when Hamp came out of the Imperial office and headed for the Piute Saloon. Wynant stood a little to one side, and very easily Hamp could have entered the saloon by pushing through one half of the two swinging doors without bothering Wynant.

The gunman made no move to step aside, and Hamp put both hands against both doors, pushed hard, and came after the opening doors. The left door struck Wynant in the chest, knocking him off balance so that he staggered back awkwardly. He straightened up, cursing, his face white, his colorless eyes receded into his head.

Hamp said to him tauntingly, "Reckon you saw me coming, mister."

Merle Wynant stood there, his left hand, the gun hand, loose at his side, his black coat thrown back, the Remington .44 with the pearl handle exposed. He opened his mouth as if to say something, and then instead of saying it, he walked past Hamp out into the street, his thin shoulders very stiff, his face set like a mask—a mask of hatred.

Lace Cordell stood at the bar, drinking with another man. He had turned his head, hearing Hamp come in, and he had watched the little scene with Merle Wynant, red coming into his wide, bronzed face.

Hamp saw him set the glass down on the bar and turn and stand with his back to the bar, elbows on the wood, watching as Hamp came up to the bar, taking a position about six feet away. Once again Hamp realized that a blow directed at one of Cordell's men was a blow at him. The Imperial Borax owner didn't like it. He hadn't liked it the last time Hamp had man-handled Wynant.

The man with Cordell, evidently an out-of-town borax buyer, from his Eastern dress, looked at Hamp curiously, and then went on speaking with Cordell.

When the bartender came up, Hamp said to him, "Beer."

It was in this bar that Hamp had shot down Rob Jensen his first night in town—a night that seemed already ages ago. This same bartender had stood behind the bar, a fat-faced, perspiring man with a semi-bald head. He said as he slid the glass of cold beer in front of Hamp, "Still in town, are you, Mr. Cameron?"

Hamp nodded.

"Workin' for Valley Borax," the bartender went on loquaciously. "Hear they're havin' a little trouble in the Valley with raiders."

"Rats," Hamp said deliberately, "who strike at night, who steal from a woman." His voice was loud and flat and it carried to every corner of the saloon. He saw Lace Cordell turn around and stare at him. The man with Cordell turned, also, surprise in his face. He was a short, fat man with a ring of reddish hair.

The Piute bartender was a little worried now, and he said hurriedly, "Too bad—too bad, Mr. Cameron." He moved away from Hamp, slapping nervously at the bar with his rag, but Hamp wouldn't let it drop there. He called after the man:

106

"Wear masks over their faces, and they're afraid to show themselves in the light of day."

He saw Lace Cordell drumming on the bar wood with his fingers, his face set tight, and he kept it up, deliberately.

"They shot down one of their own men over in Piute last night," Hamp said coolly. "Shot him from ambush without even finding out whether he was going to talk."

He saw Bill Buckley coming through the door, a frown on his gaunt face. Instead of coming up to the bar, Buckley took a chair at one of the empty card tables. The Piute Saloon at this hour of the morning was empty save for Hamp, Cordell, and his friend. Buckley picked up a deck of cards and started to shuffle them, but he was watching the play at the bar, his face expressionless now.

Lace Cordell pushed away from the bar and came over to where Hamp was standing. Putting both hands on the bar wood, he looked at Hamp coldly before speaking, and then he said tersely, "You afraid somebody won't hear you, Cameron?"

Hamp smiled at him. "Like everybody to hear it," he said.

"Everybody has heard it," Cordell snapped. "Now we'd appreciate it if you'd lower your voice. There are other men in this bar trying to converse."

He turned to go when Hamp didn't say anything at first, and then as he was moving off, Hamp called after him softly, "Maybe you don't like what I said, Cordell."

Lace Cordell stopped, his amber eyes hard, his bronzed face turning a shade deeper in color.

"Maybe I don't like the speaker, either," he said thinly.

Hamp toyed with the glass in front of him, and he looked at Cordell in the bar mirror. "You know anything about that raid on Valley wagons last night," he said, "you might want to tell Buckley about it."

"I don't know a damned thing about the raid," Cordell snapped.

Hamp shrugged. "Reckon you don't feel too bad about it, do you, Cordell? Valley Borax losing mules and wagons?"

"Why should I feel bad about it?" Cordell snapped. "I'm in business here to make money. If a competitor has hard times, Imperial Borax profits. Am I supposed to feel bad?"

"Only," Hamp smiled, "if you know anything about the raids."

Lace Cordell stood about three feet away from him at the bar. He didn't say anything at first, but Hamp saw the pulse begin to beat in his temple on the right side of his face. Behind the bar the fat-faced bartender had started to sweat profusely. The borax buyer with Cordell was staring at them, a dumb expression on his face.

Cordell was saying slowly, "You came in here looking for trouble, didn't you, Cameron?"

"Had plenty of trouble last night," Hamp observed. "Party of masked dogs burned two Valley wagons, ran off the mules. Reckon that's trouble, mister."

"And now," Cordell murmured, "you are accusing Imperial Borax of raiding Valley wagons. Is that right?"

Hamp scratched his jaw. "Wondered if you knew anything about the raids." He smiled coolly. "Only man in Mormon to profit by them, as far as I know."

"Then I'm one of the masked dogs," Cordell stated. He took off his hat and placed it on the bar. "You came here, Cameron," he repeated, "with a chip on your shoulder. You're pretty quick with a gun, and we've all seen that. Shall we see how quick you are with your fists?"

"My pleasure." Hamp smiled at him. As Cordell took off his coat, he took his off, also.

The fat bartender said worriedly, "Gentlemen, would you mind takin' it outside? Had this place wrecked before."

The borax buyer with Cordell said with amazement, "But, Mr. Cordell, you—you're a businessman!"

"This is business," Cordell told him tersely. "You're not in Chicago now, Mr. Shelby." He looked at Hamp and he said curtly, "Ready?"

"Have been," Hamp murmured, "for a long time, Cordell."

He put his coat and hat on the table where Bill Buckley was still shuffling cards, and then he walked out through the bat-wing doors. He went down the steps and into the road, and then he turned and waited.

Cordell came out, followed by the bartender and by the Eastern man, and then Sheriff Buckley eased himself through the doors, watching both of them. He called after them, "Get rid of the guns, boys."

"Don't have one," Cordell said over his shoulder.

Hamp had been unbuckling his gun belt, and he draped it across the hitch rack in front of the saloon. He was in for a tough fight, and he knew it and relished it. His loyalty now was to Valley Borax, and Cordell had been hitting at them underhandedly, striking from the dark, throwing lead from the dark, poisoning water holes in a desert country. Now he was able to hit back at a man.

Just before Cordell rushed him, however, the odd thought came to him that Lace Cordell had sounded mighty convincing when he'd denied that he'd been behind those raids. The man undoubtedly had been lying, because he could do nothing else under the circumstances, but that lie for one moment had sounded like the truth.

Cordell was slightly the shorter man, but heavier in the body, thick in the waist and the arms and the legs, and evidently a man who despite the smoothness of his hands knew how to take care of himself in a rough-and-tumble fight.

He came in with head lowered, driving both arms toward Hamp's body, hitting with his left, a pile-driving blow that nearly caved in Hamp's ribs. For a heavy man he was surprisingly quick and agile with his fists.

Straightening out, Hamp lashed back with his left fist to Cordell's face, cutting his cheekbone, but Cordell was on top of him again, a wild man in action, both fists whirling, driving Hamp back against the hitch rack.

Both men went down into the dust, both driving punches to the head. On the ground as they rolled they continued to punch, and then Hamp kicked himself free and came up to his feet, tasting blood in his mouth.

A crowd started to gather as the word spread. Men ran

from nearby saloons. They came down the alleys from the Valley and Imperial yards. Hamp spotted Stub McCoy and Steve Beaumont, the Valley yard man, running toward them, and then he saw Stuart Fleming striding down the walk, hat pulled low over his eyes. Sheila Graham had come out of the Valley office and taken a few steps in their direction, but she'd stopped now and was watching.

Lace Cordell got up from the dust, his face already grimy with blood and dirt. He came forward, his reddish-brown hair glinting in the hot morning sun, lips drawn back across his white teeth, blood trickling from the cut on his cheekbone.

Hamp lashed out and hit him full in the mouth with his right fist, splitting Cordell's lips. He tried to follow the blow with others and end the fight right there, but Cordell was far from finished. He came back with a right swing to Hamp's ear, and then drove him back into the crowd, which had now completely encircled them.

As he stumbled back, falling on hands and knees, Hamp felt a knee smashed up against the side of his head. When he looked up he saw Red Doran, the Imperial driver, staring down at him, and then little Stub McCoy tore into Doran, punching at his face, driving him back through the crowd.

Hamp had no time to watch this fight, but he did see Steve Beaumont moving forward to help Stub, and then Lace Cordell was on top of him again, his bloody, begrimed face savage with hatred, lashing out with heavy fists.

Standing flat-footed, Hamp struck back, knowing that

the time of retreating was over. They stood there in the middle of the road, under the blazing hot sun, faces grimy with dust and blood and perspiration, neither man giving ground, and the watching crowd grew silent.

Hamp took blows to the face and to the body, and he gave back blows of equal force. Through a haze of blood that started to creep across his field of vision, he saw Cordell's face, pulpy, distorted, inhuman, and he hit at that face, feeling the pain in his hands every time he connected, hoping that he was not breaking bones, but knowing that even with broken hands he had to go on hitting his man.

Then he took a step forward and he held that ground, and then he knew that he had won. A woman, watching from a second-floor window, had started to scream hysterically as it went on and on, the blows coming more slowly, but always coming, hard fists striking flesh with sickening impact.

Lace Cordell could not see after a while. He was swinging and missing and swinging again, his face a bloody smear, and then Hamp Cameron took another step forward, and another, forcing Cordell back toward the hitch rack.

It was thirty feet to the hitch rack in front of the Piute Saloon, and it took three long minutes for Hamp to pin his man against the wooden railing.

Cordell refused to go down. He kept swinging, the strength gone from his arms, unable to see, pushed back by sheer force, and then as he braced his body against the railing, it gave way and he went down.

Hamp stumbled to one side and waited. He watched

through one eye that was hazy with blood, and he saw Cordell get up on hands and knees, shaking his head like a big dog, trying to pull himself up to his feet, and unable to do so.

He waited, and then after a while he walked away and sat down on the edge of the wooden boardwalk, all the strength gone from his body. Three men went over and picked Cordell bodily from the dust of the road, carrying him toward the Imperial office, and then Stub McCoy and Steve Beaumont got their arms around Hamp and stood him up.

"Kin you walk?" Stub asked anxiously.

"Not the length of Death Valley," Hamp mumbled. "Could drink every water hole dry, though."

They helped him across the street and up an alley toward the Valley yard, and as he entered the alley he saw Sheila Graham still standing a short distance down from the Valley office. He was glad she hadn't come any closer, because it had not been pretty close up.

"Doran kicked me," Hamp murmured weakly.

"Steve an' me chased him the hell off," Stub McCoy said. "Red didn't like Steve, here, takin' a hand."

Hamp's legs gave out before they reached the wagon shed, and the two men had to carry him the remainder of the way. They sat him on a stool and stripped off his bloodied shirt. He sat there as Stub McCoy went for a bucket of water, and his face felt as if it were swelling up, getting larger and larger. He could see dimly out of one eye; the other was closed entirely. He saw Sheila Graham come into the room with towels, and he shook his head in mute protest.

Stuart Fleming came in behind Sheila, smoking a cigarette. He looked at Hamp and grimaced.

"No place for a woman," Hamp muttered. "Stub can take care of me, Miss Graham."

"You were fighting Valley Borax's fight," Sheila said calmly. "It's the least I can do."

She was not shocked by the sight of him, and he remembered, then, that she'd been raised in this business, and had probably played as a girl in the Valley Borax yard, where there had undoubtedly been fights between the tough yard men. When McCoy came back with the water, she started to wash Hamp's face.

Stuart Fleming sat down on an upturned barrel a few feet away, watching, and he said to Hamp, "What did it get you, Cameron?"

Hamp looked at him with one eye. "Satisfaction," he said.

Fleming shrugged. "You think Cordell will stop raiding Valley stations now?" he asked.

Hamp shook his head. "He knows we can be as tough as he is," he said. "That was my point in fighting him."

Stuart Fleming's smooth-shaven face reddened, and he tossed away the half-smoked cigarette angrily. "He didn't know that before, did he?" he snapped.

Hamp looked at him, a little surprised at the sudden anger in the man's voice. Fleming had pride, and his pride had been touched here.

"I don't know," Hamp murmured.

Fleming stood up, hands in his back pockets. He said tersely, "You don't think I had the nerve to go over there and fight Cordell, do you?"

Hamp shrugged. He could feel Sheila's soft fingers on his face. "Reckon I don't know that, either, mister," he said.

Stuart Fleming's face was a dull red now, and he was like a small boy in his anger, lips pouting. He said slowly, "When your face is healed, Cameron, look me up."

Sheila said quickly, "Please, Stuart. Mr. Cameron is a Valley employee now. We can't have trouble in our own company."

"I apologize," Fleming said. He looked at Hamp, and Hamp could see that he wasn't apologizing to him. His offer still stood, and it surprised Hamp. He'd begun to feel that Fleming was not nearly the man he'd been set up to be by Valley employees, and now Fleming, after seeing him batter another tough man, had openly offered to fight him. A timid man did not do that.

Fleming said almost curtly to Sheila, "See you in the office," and he went out.

"Didn't mean to rile him," Hamp murmured after the door closed behind the Valley superintendent. "He asked the questions."

"You mustn't mind Stuart." Sheila smiled. "He flies off the handle occasionally."

Hamp was looking at the floor. He said idly, "You know him pretty well."

"Very well," Sheila said, and she continued to bathe his swelling face with the moistened cloth. "I don't know what I'd have done a year ago if Stuart hadn't come along."

Hamp Cameron found himself wishing fervently that

his trail had led this way a year ago. He wondered if things would have been different.

"I'd like you and Stuart to be friends," Sheila said. "Not just for the good of the company, but for the good of yourselves."

Hamp nodded a little. She was loyal, and loyalty was one of the characteristics he admired in women as well as in men. She was standing behind Fleming, admitting his little weaknesses, but refusing to let them bother her. He said thoughtfully, "Fleming is a fortunate man having an employer like yourself, Miss Graham."

"You are just as fortunate, then," Sheila laughed lightly. "You have the same employer."

Hamp grimaced and it hurt his battered face. "There's a difference," he said.

Sheila Graham smiled again. "There is the difference," she stated, "that Stuart asked me to marry him a few days ago."

Hamp felt his heart stop beating a moment. He managed to control his voice, and it was almost casual as he spoke. He said, "What did you tell him?"

"I accepted him," Sheila said. "We are to be married this winter."

Hamp nodded. He sat there, his face hurting, his bruised, battered hands hurting, and every muscle in his body aching, crying out in fatigue, but it was nothing compared to the real hurt—the one inside, which neither soft wet towels nor soft hands could help.

Chapter Ten

Lying on a bunk in the yard bunkhouse two hours later, Hamp heard the empty borax rig rolling out. He had intended to accompany the rig, hiding in the empty wagon with the other Valley men, but Sheila Graham had absolutely forbidden it, and he had been too fatigued to object. He knew very definitely that it would be at least forty-eight hours before he would be able to move around with any degree of comfort. His other eye was almost swollen shut now, and his face was puffed out of shape. He needed two days to build up the energy he had lost in the fight with Cordell.

Steve Beaumont, who was in charge of this decoy rig, came in just before they left, giving Hamp the final details on the plan. Six men were to be with him inside the wagon. They had rigged a tarpaulin over a number of bales of hay to give the impression that they were hauling hay out to the Valley stations. The seven men were concealed under the tarpaulin.

"Be damned hot there," Beaumont grinned, "but we'll make it hotter for anybody tries to hit us."

With Stub McCoy and the swamper handling the rig, there were nine men to fight off the raiders, and Beaumont was sure they would be enough.

"We'll go as far as Furnace Creek," Beaumont explained, "third Valley station. They should hit at us before then. If not, we'll head back with a loaded rig."

After Beaumont had gone out, the company cook came in with hot coffee and some broth he had made at

Sheila Graham's suggestion. Sheila came in as he was sitting up, sipping the broth.

"I was wondering if we'd better call in Dr. Conklin," she said. "Your face is in terrible shape."

Hamp shook his head. "It'll heal up," he said.

The other wound would not heal up. Even though he had known that Fleming and Sheila Graham were close friends, it had been a shock to learn that they intended to marry very shortly. He couldn't get it out of his mind that there was something wrong with Fleming; that he was inadequate, even though the Valley superintendent had flatly offered to fight him when he was well.

There was still the paradoxical fact that Fleming thus far had done very little to stop the raids on Valley stations and wagons. He had appealed to Sheriff Buckley for help, and had let it rest there. Possibly, as an Easterner, he was doing what any Easterner would do—turning the entire matter over to the organized law. He didn't seem to know that, as honest and efficient as Bill Buckley undoubtedly was, the Sheriff of Mormon would need plenty of assistance in this case.

"I would suggest," Sheila Graham said, "that you remain here for a few days, Mr. Cameron, where you can be looked after. There are always men around the yard, and the cook can get you anything you want. I'll be close by, also, if you need me."

"Obliged." Hamp nodded. "I'll need the rest."

After she left, Bill Buckley drifted in through the door, smoking a pipe. He took a chair near the bunk and looked at Hamp thoughtfully. Then he said, "Had your fight, did you?"

"A good one." Hamp smiled. His mouth hurt when he smiled.

"Didn't figure you'd whip that *hombre*," Buckley said. "He's a rough one."

"I'm rough, too," Hamp told him.

"I know." Buckley nodded. "So now Cordell stops raidin' your wagons. Is that it?"

Hamp smiled painfully and shifted his position on the cot. He looked at Buckley out of one eye, and he said, "Reckon you know better than that, Sheriff."

"Supposin'," Buckley asked, "it wasn't Cordell. Then what?"

Hamp looked at him curiously. "It's Cordell," he said. "It has to be Cordell."

Buckley shrugged. "Maybe we'll find out this trip." He scowled. "I'll be ridin' a few miles behind that rig you boys just sent out. If there's a fight, I aim to be in it. How many men Fleming put in that wagon?"

"Nine," Hamp told him, "with the driver and swamper. They'll think twice before they hit an outfit like that."

"Idea is," Buckley told him dryly, "that they ain't supposed to know they're runnin' into trouble."

"Wish I was riding with that outfit," Hamp murmured. "Should be a good fight."

"You had enough fightin'," Buckley observed, "to last you another ten years. If there's any raiders out, we'll catch 'em."

The Sheriff of Mormon left, and Hamp closed his eyes to see if he could sleep. It was still early afternoon, the hottest part of the day. He lay on his back, still

119

stripped to the waist. Sheila Graham had left clean towels and a bucket of cold water, and constantly he wet the towel and applied it to the swellings on his face.

The bunkhouse was empty, but he could hear the blacksmith over in the smith's shop, and then two men talking just outside the door. After a while he slept—the sleep of complete exhaustion.

He wasn't sure how long he slept, but when he awoke it was dark. Someone had entered the bunkhouse to light a small oil lamp on the table in the center of the room. The door was still open and he could look through it and see stars in the sky. The heat still held.

Lifting his body, he rested himself on his elbows and looked around, his face stiff and sore. He felt of it gingerly with one hand, feeling the bruises and the cuts. His bunk was back in the shadows, and the bunkhouse was empty. He imagined that the remaining few yard men had eaten and then gone up to the main street to the various saloons.

He lay back again, wondering if he should get up and step into the cook's kitchen for something to eat. He was hungry, but the weariness still rode him, and he decided to remain on the bunk a while longer. It was then that he saw the blue barrel of a Colt gun sliding around the door, fifteen feet away, the muzzle coming to rest on himself.

For one moment he stared at the gun, and then he literally hurled himself off the bunk, his body striking the packed earth floor of the bunkhouse.

Flame spat from the mouth of the gun at the door, and the bunkhouse was filled with the roar of it. He heard the slug rip through the wall of the bunk on which he had lain, and then he leaped for his own gun belt, which he knew Stub McCoy had hung from a peg at the foot of the bunk.

He expected a second shot, but it didn't come, and then, with the Smith and Wesson in his hand, in stocking feet, he lunged toward the door. He saw the light on in the rear office of the main building, and then the door of the office opened and Sheila Graham came out. She stared toward the bunkhouse, and then came down the steps hurriedly, moving toward him.

Hamp stood outside the door, gun in hand, listening for sounds and hearing none. It was impossible to tell which way the killer had gone. The main gateway of the yard was wide open, and he could have run the short distance to the gate and got out that way, or he could have sprinted through a smaller gate on the west side of the yard that led up through an alley to the main street.

Grim-faced, breathing hard, Hamp waited for the girl to come up. He stood in the patch of light from the lamp inside, knowing that it was safe now, the attempted killer having undoubtedly left the yard.

"What happened?" Sheila asked quickly. She was breathing fast, having come toward the bunkhouse almost at a run.

"Somebody tried to put a bullet in me," Hamp told her briefly. "Figured I was sleeping."

"You—you saw him?" Sheila asked, horror in her voice.

Hamp shook his head. "Saw the gun," he explained,

"and I rolled off the bunk in time. He was gone when I got out here."

"Do you have any idea who did it?" Sheila wanted to know. "It doesn't seem possible that a man would stoop so low as to shoot you while you were asleep."

"I have an idea who did it," Hamp said tersely. He had little doubt that Merle Wynant had made his attempt to kill the man he hated, and Wynant would now have to pay the price. He'd made the gunman that promise.

Turning, he went back into the bunkhouse and started to slip into one of his clean shirts that Stub had brought down from the hotel room. Sheila Graham watched him from the doorway, and then she said slowly:

"What are you going to do?"

"A man shot at me," Hamp said simply. "I have to look him up."

"You're in no condition to go out," Sheila protested. "You need a few days of rest."

"This can't wait," Hamp said. He strapped on the gun belt and reached for his hat.

When he stepped out into the night, he saw Stuart Fleming coming up. Fleming said, "Who fired that shot?"

"When I know," Hamp told him grimly, "somebody will be dead." He walked away, heading toward the side exit and the alley leading to the main street. He figured the time now to be between eight and nine in the evening, with the saloons of Mormon jammed, the crowds spilling out into the street.

He turned into the main street, his hat pulled low over his eyes, and once again he was the pursuer, looking for a man—a man this time with a pale, thin face and hooded, colorless eyes, a man who shot from the dark and then slithered back into the darkness from which he had come.

Looking into each saloon as he passed down the street, he didn't actually expect to find Wynant. He was quite sure the gunman had left town immediately after firing that shot, but he had to make this search, just as he would make other searches for the man.

He went up one side of the long main street and then down the other, peering into each saloon, looking at the sweaty, flushed faces at each bar. When he came to the Twenty Mule Saloon he saw Wynant standing at the bar near the door, drinking alone, as usual, apparently unperturbed. Hamp stared at the man over the bat-wing doors, and then the thought came to him that either he had underestimated the killer, and Wynant was waiting calmly for him to show up, or Wynant thought he had killed his man with that shot he had fired through the open doorway of the bunkhouse.

Wynant stared at him, hatred in his eyes, as Hamp came through the door. He didn't run, though, and there was no real fear in him until Hamp stopped less than a dozen feet from him and said coldly, flatly, "Wynant, draw your gun."

The Twenty Mule Saloon was jammed, every space at the bar taken, every card table filled, with men pushing in and out through the doors behind Hamp.

Merle Wynant looked at him, his face becoming waxy, eyes receding into his head.

"What?" he asked weakly.

"Draw your gun," Hamp repeated.

The crowd nearby was suddenly conscious of the fact that a gun fight was impending. The men at the bar moved out of the way hurriedly. A nearby card table emptied, a bottle of liquor spilling at Hamp's feet. He stood there, watching Wynant, waiting for the first tell-tale movement that would give him the right to draw his gun and fire, but Wynant had frozen at the bar. One elbow was on the wood and the other hand was hanging at his side—the left hand, his gun hand. His black coat was open, and the pearl-handled Remington .44 was in the clear.

Very suddenly it became quiet in the Twenty Mule Saloon, but outside on the walk and on the porch of the saloon the noise continued, loud, boisterous voices. A piano tinkled in the Death Valley Saloon next door. A man came in through the doors behind Hamp, talking loudly, and then he stopped suddenly, as if an iron hand had been clamped around his throat.

A drunk in the far corner of the saloon, standing against the wall, head lolling, was muttering to himself, unseeing, only semiconscious.

Hamp Cameron said again, "Draw your gun, Wynant."

Then the door squeaked behind him, and a man whooped in a drunken voice, "Hurray fer President Garfield!"

Hamp staggered as the drunk lurched into him from behind, and in that moment Merle Wynant broke for the side door, running the whole length of the bar.

Recovering, Hamp went after him, tearing around an

empty card table. His boot struck one of the legs of the table and he lurched forward, falling awkwardly, the side of his head striking a nearby chair.

He rolled over, stunned for the moment, and he sat there on the floor, shaking his head, until two men in the saloon helped him to his feet and up to the bar. The bartender pushed a glass of whisky toward him, and he drank some of it, his head clearing.

"Bad fall," the bartender said. "You all right now, mister?"

"All right," Hamp said. He put a coin on the bar to pay for the drink, and then he turned and went out, knowing that it was useless to search for Wynant anymore tonight. He'd been in bad shape, physically, when he left the Valley yard, and he was in worse shape now after the fall.

He walked back to the Valley yard, entered the bunkhouse, and sat down on the edge of his bunk. He was still a little puzzled at Wynant's behavior. The gunman had acted as if he had been surprised by Hamp's visit, even though Hamp had definitely told him he'd go after him if he shot from cover. Wynant would not have forgotten that threat, and yet he had not run, and he'd been drinking calmly at a Mormon bar almost as if he had not fired that shot!

He had fired it, though, Hamp told himself. No other man in Mormon, excepting Lace Cordell, would want him dead so badly, and Cordell had been in no condition this evening to be hunting an enemy. Besides, Wynant was Cordell's hired gun hand, paid to liquidate Imperial Borax enemies. He'd fired the shot, and yet there was that small worm of doubt in Hamp Cameron's mind as he kicked off his boots and lay back on the bunk.

Chapter Eleven

At high noon the next day, as Hamp was eating in the Valley Borax bunkhouse, a Valley rig rolled into the yard with the word that Steve Beaumont's decoy wagon had reached Devil's Hole station and was pushing on into the Valley without having sighted any raiders.

Hamp finished his coffee and then left the bunkhouse to step into the office. He found Sheila Graham and Stuart Fleming talking with the driver. Fleming looked at Hamp with little pleasure as he came in, and then he said, "Looks like they're not going to attack that outfit."

Hamp frowned. "Sheriff Buckley come back?" he asked.

Fleming looked at him. "Buckley out in the Valley?"

"Told me he'd follow the rig at a distance," Hamp explained, "so he'd be in on the fight when it started."

"In a way, I'm glad there was no raid," Sheila murmured. "Maybe it will stop now."

Hamp shook his head. "Can't stop once it's started," he told her. "Too much money involved here. The man who controls the borax industry in Death Valley stands to make millions. They'll hit again." He looked at Stuart Fleming, who was sitting on the edge of a desk, lighting a cigar, and he said, "What do you think, Fleming?"

Fleming shrugged. "This crowd might strike on the other side of Devil's Hole," he pointed out. "Beaumont promised to send a fast rider back after they reach Fur-

126

nace Creek station. We'll know then."

"Reckon we won't know any more then," Hamp scowled, "than we know now. The way it looks to me, this bunch is steering clear of that rig. They know what's in it."

"How would they know?" Fleming asked. "We kept it quiet in the yard here. None of the yard men even knew about it until the wagon rolled out of the yard. Beaumont saw to that."

"They still know," Hamp told him grimly. "They'd have hit us by this time if they didn't."

He didn't tell Sheila Graham, but he was positive the attack would come now from another quarter. Another Valley Borax rig would be hit, or another station raided and the mules run off into the mountains. The bleeding process would continue until Valley Borax could bleed no more, and then, hopelessly in debt and unable to run the processed borax out of Death Valley, Sheila Graham would have to sell or go out of business, leaving the field to Lace Cordell.

"I've sent one extra man out to each station in the Valley," Fleming said. "That's the best we can do for the present. I realize it's not adequate."

"I have hopes," Sheila stated, "that Sheriff Buckley will eventually apprehend them."

Fleming said to Hamp through a cloud of cigar smoke, "What are your plans, Cameron?"

Hamp pursed his lips. "Figured I'd take another ride into the Valley," he said. He saw Sheila look at him quickly.

"Are you well enough?" she asked.

Hamp felt of his still puffed face. It was stiff and sore, but he had slept well the previous night after returning from the chase of Merle Wynant. He said, "I'll be all right, ma'am." He added, "Going back to the hotel now. You'll know where to find me."

He went out then, leaving them together, and he was still in a bad mood because Buckley's scheme had failed. During the early-afternoon hours he sat on the hotel porch, smoking, considering the matter. In some way word had been sent into the Valley or to Piute City that the rig leaving Mormon was not empty, as it appeared to be, and was not to be attacked. How they had learned that fact was something else, unless Cordell's raiders had a spy working for Valley Borax, someone who was in the inner circle.

At five o'clock in the evening Sheriff Bill Buckley rode in, hot, dusty, somber. Hamp watched him dismount in front of his office and step inside, and then he got up from the porch and crossed the road. He found Buckley in the rear of the office, dousing his face in a bucket of water.

Buckley looked at him and shook his head in disgust.

"How far did you go?" Hamp asked him.

"Halfway to Furnace Creek," Buckley stated. "They ain't hittin' that outfit, Cameron. They had plenty o' chances all the way out if they wanted to do any damage. That one they let go through."

"Why?" Hamp asked softly.

Bill Buckley wiped his face with a towel. "Reckon you know the answer to that one as well as I do," he murmured.

"All right," Hamp said. "They knew what was in that wagon, but how?"

"Been tryin' to figure that out all the way in here," Buckley told him. "Wasn't too many people knew about it."

"Just the ones who were in the office," Hamp observed, "when you thought of the idea—Sheila Graham, Fleming, Stub McCoy, Beaumont, you, and myself."

Sheriff Buckley sat down on a stool, the towel in his hand, his sandy hair mussed, eyes still red from the ride through part of the Valley. "Wasn't Sheila," he mused, "an' I don't think it was McCoy or Beaumont. Both them boys worked for Charlie Graham. They're good Valley Borax men."

Hamp stared down at him, lips tight. "Doesn't leave many others," he said evenly. "It leaves Stuart Fleming." As he said it, his mind started to click. Fleming had done very little to stop Lace Cordell's raids on Valley wagons and stations. He'd been content to sit back and let Valley take the beating—possibly for a reason! Possibly because he, too, was Cordell's man!

"Leaves Fleming," Bill Buckley was saying idly, "an' you an' me."

Hamp laughed grimly. "If Fleming has switched over to Cordell," he said tersely, "it would be a very easy matter for him to run Valley Borax into bankruptcy. He can just sit back and wait, and do nothing."

"I figure he's tryin' to do somethin'," Buckley protested. "Always had the idea Fleming was all right. Hell of a thing to say that Fleming was workin' against

129

the girl he's goin' to marry."

"He may have made a deal with Cordell," Hamp said flatly, "to turn over Valley Borax to him, and then both of them control the entire borax industry. Do you think a piece of bait like that would attract Fleming?"

Buckley shrugged. "Attract plenty o' men," he observed, "not just Fleming, but it still don't make sense, Cameron. If he's marryin' Sheila Graham, he takes over Valley Borax anyway."

"He knows Valley is on the rocks, financially," Hamp told him, "and that Cordell can put them out of business. His best bet is to string along with Cordell, which Sheila will not do. Besides, he hasn't married Sheila yet."

Bill Buckley put down the towel and walked over to his battered roll-top desk to take a cigar from the box there. He said over his shoulder, "You got it all figured out, mister, but you got no proof. Fleming has a good reputation in this town. I don't have a single thing against him."

"Will you watch him?" Hamp asked. "Watch every move he makes?"

"Reckon I'll do that," Buckley said. "Watchin' everybody in this town." He added sourly, "I'm the law in this town, an' I don't like it that there's so much lawbreakin'. I'll watch everybody. I'll watch you, too, friend."

Hamp smiled at him, and then pointed to his still swollen and bruised face. "This look like I'm Cordell's man?" he asked.

"Hell," Buckley growled. "Does everybody have to throw in with Cordell?"

"He's the power in the Valley right now," Hamp said. "He stands to gain the most if Valley Borax closes up."

As he moved toward the door to the street, Buckley called after him, "Where in hell you goin' now, Cameron? I should know what's goin' on around here."

"Figured I'd ride up to Piute City," Hamp told him.

Buckley frowned. "There's a place to keep away from," he said. "What do you expect to find up there?"

"For one thing," Hamp smiled, "maybe the man who threw lead at me through the doorway of the Valley bunkhouse last night when I was supposed to be sleeping. Maybe other things."

"Maybe," Bill Buckley warned him, "a bellyful of hot lead. If Manuel's is the hideout fer that band o' raiders, they'll know now that you're a Valley Borax man."

Hamp stepped back into the room to pick up a cigar from the open cigar box on the desk. He put it in his mouth and he said softly, "I have friends in Piute City, Sheriff."

Buckley scowled at him. "Never seen a man make friends an' enemies as quick as you, mister. Just walk easy over there."

Hamp went out, walking back to the Valley yard. He had his supper in the mess hall, and then he saddled the big buckskin he had ridden his first day in the Valley. No one took any particular notice of him as he rode through the alley up to the main street and then headed toward Wind Gap.

It was dusk when he rode out of town, following the graded road that led into Wind Gap. When he reached the gap, however, he turned off on the old stage road that led north and east through the hills to Piute City. He could feel the air growing cooler as he moved up into the Funeral Range, and it was a welcome relief after the heat of the long day in Mormon.

A slim sliver of moon came up the ridge of mountains ahead of him, lighting up the road, which still seemed to be in fairly good condition. The buckskin had been stabled all during the day, and was anxious to run a little. Hamp gave the big animal free rein, and the buckskin ran down the miles. They raised the lights of Piute City at about ten or eleven o'clock in the evening, and then Hamp drew up on a summit overlooking the old mining town.

Dismounting for a few minutes, he squatted on his heels just off the road, rolling. a cigarette, letting the buckskin breathe, and then he rode on again, turning off the stage road and swinging around to the rear of the tumble-down shacks along the main street, coming up behind the sheds of Manuel's Casino.

He tied the buckskin behind the sheds and then moved forward on foot, coming up to the rear door of the big building, the doorway that led to the kitchen in which he had eaten the tortillas and beans Rita Sánchez had prepared for him.

There were a number of horses at the hitch rack in front of the building, and several more tied in the sheds. He could hear them stamping as he came up to the door. There was a light in the kitchen, and he stepped to the window to look in before entering. He saw Rita Sánchez just coming through the door from the barroom. She was alone, and he tapped gently on the windowpane to attract her attention.

She came to the door immediately, showing no alarm. When she opened the door and stood in the patch of yellow lamplight, tall and slender against the light, Hamp called softly, "Over here, Rita."

She walked over to where he was standing in the shadows, and she said thoughtfully, "It is you, Señor Cameron."

"You know my name," Hamp murmured.

"You are a Valley Borax man," Rita Sánchez said slowly, "and this is a dangerous place for you to be. You are aware of that?"

"Reckon that's the reason I came the back way." Hamp grinned. "Looking for another man."

"The last man you looked for died very quickly," Rita told him. "It is not good to be the man for whom you look."

"Still trying to learn who fired that shot," Hamp told her. "I wanted Piute Charlie alive. He was no good to us dead."

"Few men are," Rita murmured. "Who is this man you want now?"

"Dark, slim man with a narrow face," Hamp told her. "He was here the other night when I met you."

"He is the man who shot Piute Charlie?" Rita asked.

Hamp nodded. "Tried to kill me the other night, also. Figured I'd look him up out here."

"That man is not here now," Rita told him.

Hamp looked at her. "Reckon I could wait," he murmured. He saw the girl shake her head in mild exasperation, and then she said:

"Men are too anxious to die, and too anxious to kill, señor. It is not good."

"One thing a man can't do," Hamp said softly. "He can't run. When a man shoots at him in the dark, he must look for that man or expect more shots from the dark until he's dead."

Rita Sánchez nodded soberly. "You may wait inside," she stated. "You can watch the bar through a crack in the door."

"I am obliged to you," Hamp told her.

"I hope when you find this man," Rita murmured, "you do not die."

"I don't aim to die." Hamp smiled. He followed her into the kitchen and took a chair over toward the door. Then he watched Rita walk to the kitchen table and turn down the wick of the lamp, and then blow it out. She went past him then, through the door to the bar, leaving it slightly ajar when she went out.

He sat in the darkness looking out through the crack, and from this position he could view the entire length of the bar. There were at least a dozen men at the bar, and some of them he recognized from his previous visit here. Merle Wynant was not in the Casino.

Hamp shifted his position so that he could see the card tables, also, and then he sat back in the chair to watch through the crevice. Manuel and Rita worked behind the bar, Rita always cool and unperturbed, smiling slightly at the witticisms of the men at the bar.

The breeds watched her silently, intently, their black eyes following every movement. One of them who had been drinking heavily reached out his hand to her as she went by on one occasion, and then a tall, blond-haired man with a red, pock-marked face slipped his gun out of his holster in one long, easy motion and slammed the barrel of the gun across the breed's arm.

The breed let out a yelp of pain and stumbled away. The blond man put the gun back in the holster, touched his hat to Rita Sánchez, and without a word went on drinking.

Hamp smiled a little, remembering Rita's statement that she had friends in these hills. There were men here who had their brand of respect for her.

The silent men drifted in and out of the Casino, having their drinks, sometimes talking with an acquaintance for a few minutes, but always on the alert, always watching the door. These were the men who lived in the shadows with the law always one step behind them, or with an enemy ready to send a bullet crashing from the darkness.

For an hour Hamp sat by the door, watching, wondering if he was wasting his time here, wondering if Wynant had left the country altogether, and then a man came through the door and stepped up to the bar, and he knew his time had not been wasted. The man was Stuart Fleming.

Hamp stared at the tall, smooth-shaven Valley Borax superintendent. Fleming had his drink at the bar, nodding to Rita casually, having a few words with her, smiling and leaning forward over the bar, and in that moment Hamp knew that Fleming had been here before—many times before—and that possibly he was one of the "friends" of Rita Sánchez.

He sat on the edge of the chair, staring at Fleming, a frown on his face. Fleming was engaged to Sheila Graham, and yet he had been coming over here to see Rita. Possibly, also, there were other reasons why he'd come to Piute City—possibly to arrange for raids against his own wagons and stations, possibly to pass on information to Cordell's hired gun hands that one particular rig, in which a half-dozen tough Valley men were hiding, was to be left alone.

As he sat watching Fleming, he wondered if Rita would tell him that another Valley Borax man was on the premises. He hoped that she wouldn't, because he wanted to watch Fleming.

After a while Rita left him to serve another drinker, and as Fleming didn't look toward the door, he was quite sure Rita had not said anything. In a few minutes Rita came through the door, closing it behind her, and she stood in the shadows in front of him.

Hamp said, "No luck."

"He may not come tonight," Rita told him. "There is another Valley Borax man here. You, of course, know Señor Fleming?"

"I know him," Hamp said briefly.

"Is he to know that you are here?" Rita Sánchez asked.

"No." Hamp smiled. "It would be better if he didn't."

"You do not trust him?" Rita said slowly.

"Why is he here?" Hamp asked.

Rita paused before replying, and then she said, "I do not ask men why they come to the Casino to drink. That is not good."

"You know why I'm here," Hamp observed.

Rita put a hand on his shoulder. She said softly, "You do not belong here, Señor Cameron."

Hamp took her hand and held it for a moment, remembering that Sheila Graham was to marry Stuart Fleming. She had told him that. He was a fool, therefore, to remain faithful to a woman who was not for him. He said slowly, "You have to leave right away?"

"Only," Rita Sánchez murmured, "if the other woman is worth it."

Hamp hesitated, and then the Mexican girl withdrew her hand. She said softly, "I know." Then she went back to the bar.

Hamp watched her through the crack in the door, and once again he felt ashamed of himself. He noticed that Stuart Fleming was gone, and it was then that he heard the door open softly behind him, and someone come in.

Chapter Twelve

Very gently, Hamp Cameron drew the Smith and Wesson and held it in his hand. He turned slowly in the darkness until he was facing the door, but he didn't get up from the chair. He could see the dim outline of the doorway that opened on the rear of the Casino, but he couldn't see the man standing by the doorway. He apparently hadn't moved after he had come in, and Hamp was not sure on which side of the doorway he was standing.

The gun tight in his hand, Hamp waited for him to make a move. He remembered that Fleming had left the bar, and there was the possibility that he had come around to the rear of the Casino and entered the back door with the intention of seeing Rita Sánchez privately.

Whoever the man was, Hamp was positive he had seen him when he had come through the door, and then quickly stepped back against the wall. He was waiting now, probably with drawn gun, also, waiting for Hamp to reveal himself, unwilling, also, to let Hamp know who he was.

Steadying the gun, Hamp made no move, no sound. If the man who had come in was Merle Wynant, it meant he'd have to open fire the moment this fact became known. Wynant would fire at him without hesitation.

Outside at the bar they could hear the clink of glasses, and occasionally the low hum of talk. In the kitchen there were no sounds. A full minute passed, and then another, with neither man making a move, and then without warning the man who had been standing near the door opened it and went out into the night.

Hamp had only a quick glimpse of him against the outline of the door, but he was positive the man was not Merle Wynant. This man had been pretty big—as big as Stuart Fleming.

Then the door from the barroom opened quickly and Rita Sánchez came in. She said, "You must leave, Señor Cameron, at once."

Hamp stood up, holstering the gun. "What happened?" he asked.

"You have your horse in the rear?" Rita asked him, ignoring the question.

"Behind the sheds." Hamp nodded.

"They'll be waiting for you if you go out that way," Rita told him tensely. "You must leave by the front door. Walk out of this kitchen calmly, and then leave by the front door. Take any horse at the rack and ride fast—as fast as you can."

"Reckon I can't steal another man's horse," Hamp protested.

"You'll be dead in ten minutes if you do not," Rita warned him. "A horse means nothing in these hills. The horse you take will be one that was stolen from another. Now hurry."

"Just one question," Hamp said quietly. "Who in hell am I running from, Rita?"

"I do not know," Rita confessed. "I saw these men over the bar doors. There were five of them out in the shadows of the street. They rode up, and another man spoke to them. Then they moved around toward the sheds. I am sure they were coming to look for you."

"Was the man who spoke to them Stuart Fleming?" Hamp persisted.

Rita Sánchez hesitated. "I do not know," she said, and Hamp Cameron could not tell if she was lying or telling the truth.

She left immediately, and then he walked out into the barroom, his lips pursed in a soundless whistle. He walked past the bar and then toward the door.

Several men at the bar glanced at him quickly, and one man dropped his hand toward his gun. Hamp just looked at him, smiled a little, and kept going. He pushed out through the doors, crossed the porch, and went down the steps.

139

There were seven horses at the hitch rack. He walked over to a chestnut with a white face, slipped the reins, and then mounted. As he was swinging the chestnut away from the rack, he heard men running from the direction of the sheds to the rear.

A man yelled sharply, "There he goes!"

A gun boomed as Hamp bent low in the saddle and tore up the street. Other guns opened up behind him, and he could hear the lead flying past, and then the chestnut gave a sudden, desperate surge forward.

Hamp kicked the stirrups loose, knowing she'd been hit, and when the big animal stumbled and went down, he flew clear, landing on hands and knees, rolling, his body relaxed.

When he came up, he heard the shouts of triumph behind him, and then more bullets. He counted six men running toward him, firing as they came, and then he ran toward one of the tumble-down shacks on the right side of the road.

From the open doorway of the building he stopped to send three quick shots at his pursuers, stopping them, sending one man to his knees, and then he ran into the building, feeling the rotting boards give way beneath his steps.

There was a window on the other side of the shack, and he scrambled through the window, falling to the ground on the other side. As he raced down through the high brush along the rear of the buildings he could hear a man saying calmly, "Get around to the rear. Cut him off."

The voice was strangely familiar, but he could not

definitely place it. It could have been Fleming, but he was not positive. The night did tricks with a man's voice.

They were coming down on either side of the building, and they had been ordered to cut him off, to cut him down. Tearing through the brush, Hamp came up at the rear of another building, stepping in through a door that was hanging from one hinge.

He heard a rat scurrying away as he entered the building, once more moving through it, this time to the front door. A man was just entering the building out of which be had come. He waited until the road was clear, and then he stepped out and crossed quickly to the opposite side of the street, entering another abandoned building, a saloon.

As he crossed the road this time he looked in the direction of the Casino, and he saw a small group of men on the porch, staring in his direction. He was positive, however, that they could not see him.

The saloon building was a two-story structure, and Hamp waited until his eyes had become accustomed to this greater darkness inside, and then he located the stairway and went up the steps to the second floor, feeling his way carefully. The stair boards creaked beneath his weight, and he tested each one before putting his full weight upon it, not wanting the noise of collapsing stairs attracting the attention of the men across the road, still searching the first shack into which he had gone.

At the head of the stairs he turned left, walking along a darkened corridor, and then stepped into one of the rooms facing the main street. Feeling his way across the room, around a bed and a table, he stepped to the window to look out, and then he straightened up suddenly, aware of the fact that something was wrong here.

In feeling his way around the bed, his hands had come in contact with blankets. In an abandoned house like this, the blankets should have been damp, mildewed, gritty and dirty with falling plaster from the ceiling. The blankets with which his hands had come in contact were dry, and they felt clean. They had undoubtedly been in use, which meant that this particular room was occupied.

Standing against the wall, Hamp drew the gun he had holstered as he started up the stairs. He listened carefully, positive now that he heard someone breathing in the room. The bed had been empty, he was sure of that, but he was just as sure now that this room was not empty.

He stood back against the wall, listening, peering into the shadows, and then a man said from the opposite wall less than twelve feet from where he stood, "Nothin' to worry about in here, Jack. I'm runnin' too."

"Who's this?" Hamp asked softly. He kept his gun raised as he saw a man coming out of the shadows, moving toward him.

"Reckon you walked right into my house," the stranger chuckled. "Been watchin' the whole business from the window. Damn smart o' you to cross over an' come in here when they're searchin' the other side o' the street."

Hamp put his gun away. Looking out through the

cracked window, he could see shadowy figures moving around across the road, and he could hear their muffled voices.

"Law after you, mister?" the man in the room asked.

Hamp laughed shortly. "Law of the strong," he said tersely.

The other man considered this for a moment. "You'd o' made it," he observed, "if they hadn't got yore horse."

Hamp didn't say anything to that. He watched the men below moving on to the next house, and then he understood their plan. They intended to search every abandoned house in town; they were going to track him down like a wild animal until they found him.

"You hiding out here?" he asked the fellow.

"Livin' here," the man told him. "Ain't bad. Plenty private."

"Won't be private too long," Hamp told him. "They'll be coming this way once they reach the end of the street and start down the other side."

"Reckon we better git out." The man laughed. "I ain't aimin' to be shot fer you, mister."

Hamp heard him move across the room to the bed and start to roll the blanket.

"What are you running from?" Hamp asked him.

There was a pause, and then the man's voice came back at him, dry, caustic. "From El Paso, Texas. Reckon I didn't ask you why they was chasin' you."

"All right." Hamp smiled. He'd labeled the man as another drifter who had broken with the law and now had to live away from it the remainder of his life.

143

"Safest place in this town tonight," he said, "is Manuel's Casino. I'm riding out, myself."

"Have another horse?" the man asked curiously. He was waiting by the door now, having gathered his few possessions.

"I have a horse," Hamp told him.

They went down the stairs together, feeling their way carefully, Hamp still unable to get a look at his friend.

As they were crossing the floor of the saloon toward the rear door, Hamp said softly, "You going to Manuel's?"

"Ridin' out," the fugitive said briefly. "Been here a month, an' it's hell. Have to find someplace else now." He spoke soberly, glumly, hopelessness in his voice, and Hamp said to him quietly, "Here's a little advice, mister."

"What's that?" the man asked.

"Go back to El Paso," Hamp told him. "Stand up to it."

"Not me." The fugitive scowled. "Rather go straight to hell, friend."

They walked toward the doorway that Hamp could see dimly ahead of them, a patch of light against the deeper shadows, and then he had his first good look at his new found friend as he stepped into the entranceway. The man was tall, about his own height and of his general build. He wore a flat-crowned hat and he carried his saddle roll under his left arm.

As he stepped into the doorway a gun roared from the shadows outside. Hamp, a few feet behind the fugitive, saw the spurt of orange flame and heard the man ahead of him gasp as he staggered.

Catching him with his left arm, Hamp slid the Smith and Wesson from the holster and fired twice. A man lurched out of the shadows and fell to his hands and knees less than six feet from the doorway.

Holstering the gun, Hamp lowered the wounded man to the floor. The body was limp in his arms, and he was wondering if the man were already dead when he spoke. The fugitive said softly, a note of pathos in his voice, "Goin' back to El Paso, mister."

Hamp was sure he was dead when his body reached the floor, but there was no time to wait to make sure. He could hear voices in the street behind him, and a man was calling sharply, "This way! This way!"

Again, it was that hauntingly familiar voice, and as Hamp leaped out through the doorway, past the man he had shot, who was still on hands and knees, he tried desperately to remember where he had heard that voice. Stuart Fleming was in town; there was the possibility that Lace Cordell and Merle Wynant were in the vicinity, also. Cordell could have followed him here, having seen him leaving Mormon. He could not be sure, though, that it was Cordell's voice, or Fleming's voice.

Running through weed-grown back yards along the main street, he headed back toward the Casino, coming up behind the sheds where he had tied the buckskin earlier in the evening. Behind him he left a man who had died in his place—a man whose face he had never seen and whose name he did not know, but a man who had been mistaken for himself and who had paid the full penalty.

It was a sobering thought. Heading west into the hills away from Mormon, and away from the stage road to Mormon, Hamp considered the fact that tonight armed men had ruthlessly sought to kill him. They had gone about it coldly and calmly, and they were still searching for him. If it had not been for the fugitive who had walked out of the building ahead of him, he would have been dead at this moment instead of riding through the hills toward Death Valley and the Devil's Hole Station.

The sun was coming up when Hamp dismounted in front of the horse sheds. A sleepy-eyed hostler came out to look at him and scratch his head.

Hamp had breakfast with them and then turned in for a few hours' sleep. It was noon when he awoke. A borax rig had rolled in and the mules were being changed. Outside, he could hear Stub McCoy and Steve Beaumont talking with the attendants.

When he came outside, blinking in the brassy sunshine, Stub came over and shook his hand.

"Reckon you're lookin' a hell of a lot better than the last time we saw you," little Stub chuckled. "Boys here told us you'd ridden in early this mornin'."

Steve Beaumont shook hands with him, also. The big Valley yard man said glumly, "Had a hot ride out to Furnace Creek, Hamp. Nothin' else. Didn't see a sign of raiders. What do you make of it?"

"They knew you were in that wagon," Hamp told him. "They let it alone."

"How?" Beaumont scowled. "Wasn't anybody in town knew we had our boys inside. Had a tarpaulin over the top an' the boys was underneath it. You figure we

146

got a spy in the yard, Hamp?"

Hamp drew them aside, out of hearing of the two station attendants, and then he told them of his experiences in Piute City.

When he had finished, Stub McCoy said slowly, "You saw Fleming in Manuel's, Hamp?"

"He was there," Hamp nodded, "and I got the impression that he'd been there before—many times."

"What in hell would he be doin' in Piute City?" Steve Beaumont muttered.

"Maybe," Stub said, "the same thing Hamp was doin'. Lookin' around. Tryin' to learn somethin'."

Hamp didn't say anything to that. He rolled a cigarette, lighted it, and watched the attendants hooking the teams of mules to the chain.

"You don't know who was chasin' you all over town," Steve Beaumont said. "Reckon you didn't see any of 'em."

Hamp shook his head. "Too dark," he said briefly. He didn't tell them that the man who had led the bunch had a voice that had been familiar to him, but which he could not identify.

"Fleming will tell us what he was doin' in Piute," Stub McCoy said confidently. "Maybe he even saw some of 'em was chasin' you, Hamp."

Hamp Cameron smiled faintly. "We're not telling Fleming I saw him in Piute," he said quietly.

Both Steve Beaumont and Stub McCoy stared at him. Stub was the first to find his voice, the full implication of Hamp's statement finally sinking in.

"No?" he said weakly.

"No," Hamp told him. "Not until we know more than we do. From now on we keep our mouths shut and our eyes and ears open."

"A man lives longer that way," McCoy said thoughtfully.

Chapter Thirteen

It was past nine o'clock in the evening when the rig rolled into Mormon, Stub McCoy riding the near wheeler, Steve Beaumont handling the tandem, and Hamp riding the buckskin. Stub took the rig directly to the railroad siding, but Hamp turned off, dismounting in front of the Valley Borax office when he saw the light inside.

Tying the buckskin to the rail, he saw Stuart Fleming step out of the Twenty Mule Saloon and cross the road toward him. He waited on the walk until Fleming came up, and he listened carefully when the Valley superintendent spoke, trying to remember if this were the voice he had heard in Piute City the previous night.

"Kind of changed your plans," Fleming observed. "Buckley told me you were riding up to Piute, and now you come out of Death Valley with one of our rigs."

"I was in Piute," Hamp told him, and he could make nothing from the sound of the voice. From a distance, and under peculiar circumstances, voices sounded different. Fleming might or might not have been the man who had led the killers after him, but he did know that Hamp had been in Piute.

"Learn anything?" Fleming wanted to know.

148

"Only," Hamp smiled grimly, "that's it's a damned good place to keep away from."

He looked at Fleming steadily as he said this, but the blond man's face showed nothing.

Fleming said casually, "Could have told you that, Cameron."

"What do you know about Piute?" Hamp asked him.

"I've been there," Fleming said evenly. "I know Manuel."

"And Rita Sánchez?" Hamp murmured.

He saw Fleming's lips tighten, and the Valley superintendent glanced toward the door of the office.

"And Rita Sánchez," Fleming agreed. "Maybe I've been in Piute for the same reason that you have."

"I didn't learn anything," Hamp told him, "and I rode over to our Devil's Hole station to meet up with Stub McCoy and Beaumont on the way in."

"The wagon wasn't hit, then?" Fleming asked.

"No," Hamp said. "They let it alone."

He didn't say anything about the fight in Piute City, and he noticed that Fleming didn't admit that he had been there the previous night, either.

As they walked toward the door of the office, Hamp felt the conviction growing upon him that Stuart Fleming was a man who would have to be watched. There were too many loose ends to his story, too many questions unanswered in Hamp's mind.

In the office they found Sheriff Buckley talking with Sheila Graham. Buckley stood up when they came in. He looked at Hamp critically, and then said, "You got back all right, did you?"

149

"I got back." Hamp smiled.

"Had a mind to ride after you last night." Buckley scowled. "Run into any trouble up there?"

"Had a little lead thrown at me," Hamp told him. "I headed into the Valley and stayed over at our Devil's Hole station."

He looked at Sheila and he saw the concern in her eyes. Fleming had taken a seat in an empty chair in the room. He hadn't said anything, but he was listening carefully.

"You learn anything?" Buckley asked Hamp.

Hamp shook his head.

Sheila said quietly, "I wouldn't advise your riding into Piute City too often, Hamp. If the raiders are coming from that point, you may be in serious trouble."

"Tell that to your superintendent, also," Hamp said evenly.

From the way Sheila looked at Stuart Fleming, he realized she was unaware of the fact that Fleming had ever been over to the abandoned mining town at all.

"I've had a look around there once or twice," Fleming stated calmly, and Hamp saw Bill Buckley glance at him sharply.

"More people over in Piute these days," Buckley grumbled, "than in Mormon."

"I'll have to ask all of you to be more careful in the future," Sheila said. "I do not want anyone killed."

"Man killed over in Piute City last night," Hamp told her. "Supposed to be me they shot."

"How's that?" Bill Buckley asked sharply.

Hamp told him of the drifter who had walked into the

150

bullet as he went out of the back door of the abandoned saloon. As he spoke he looked at Stuart Fleming, who was listening intently. Fleming's face showed nothing.

Bill Buckley said when Hamp finished, "Reckon they're playing fer keeps, Cameron. I'll have to ask you to stay out o' that town unless you go in with me."

Hamp smiled at him. "Just as easy to shoot at two men from a dark alley as one," he observed.

Sheila Graham looked at Bill Buckley. "After hearing this," she said slowly, "I feel almost inclined to sell out and leave the Valley."

"You can't run," Hamp told her, "once you're in a thing. You have men with this company who worked for your father. Men like McCoy and Beaumont. They're loyal to Valley Borax. You sell them when you sell the company."

Neither Buckley nor Fleming said anything, and they sat there for several long moments in silence, and then Sheila Graham said, "I'll consider it a while longer."

"Right back where we started," Bill Buckley growled. "Nothin' come o' my scheme to run a decoy wagon into the Valley. What do you have in mind, Cameron?"

Hamp shrugged and shook his head. He had no intention of again revealing to Stuart Fleming what his plans would be in the future.

Buckley said to Fleming, "Reckon you better keep an extra guard with every wagon goin' out, even if you have to close up your yard to do it. A yard ain't no good unless you're takin' borax out o' the Valley."

"I've made those arrangements," Fleming said.

Sheriff Buckley stood up. He said to Hamp, "Buy you

a drink, Cameron. I want to hear more about that fight in Piute City."

Hamp went out with him, and as they were crossing the road he said quietly, "Fleming was in Piute last night just before that bunch jumped me."

Bill Buckley stopped and looked at him. Then he said slowly, "You still stringin' along with the idea that Fleming's in with Cordell?"

Hamp shrugged. "Add it all up," he said tersely. "Fleming does nothing to stop the raids; when we send a decoy wagon out into the Valley, the raiders don't touch it, and Fleming is one of the few people who knew about the ruse. Now a few minutes after I see him in Piute this bunch jumps me. What do you make of it?"

"Hell of a lot o' coincidences," Buckley agreed, "but it still could mean nothin'. If you spotted him with this bunch in Piute we'd have somethin'."

"Reckon I can't say I saw him," Hamp admitted. "I heard a man call several times, and the voices sounded familiar."

"Like Fleming?" Buckley asked.

Hamp shook his head. "I'm not sure. It could have been."

"Can't hang a man on that," Buckley told him.

"I aim to watch him, though," Hamp said grimly. "I figure on watching every move he makes from now on."

They entered the Piute Saloon, and as they stepped to the bar, Buckley said, "What's your next move? Figured you had somethin' in mind back there, but didn't want Fleming to hear it."

Hamp nodded. He said softly, "About time Imperial Borax did a little worrying about getting borax out of the Valley."

Buckley ordered drinks and then pushed his hat back on his head. "You aim to give Cordell a taste o' his own medicine?" he asked.

Hamp smiled. "You're the law in this town," he said. "Reckon I can't admit that, Sheriff, but if I were Cordell I'd have an escort with every borax rig coming in and going out of Mormon."

Buckley frowned. "You raiding his wagons?" he asked. Hamp smiled. "Be no shooting," he promised, "at men or mules."

As he was having his drink he saw Lace Cordell coming through the door, and it was the first time he had seen the Imperial owner since the day of the fight. Cordell's face was coming back into shape, but there were still purple bruises and scars, some of which would never leave him.

Cordell saw him, and his amber eyes hardened. He looked away as he stepped up to the bar some distance to the right of where Hamp stood with Bill Buckley.

Hamp said to Buckley, "You seen Wynant around?"

Sheriff Buckley shook his head. "Not the last few days," he said.

Lace Cordell was walking over to an empty card table with a bottle and a glass, and Hamp watched him, waiting until he sat down. Then he nodded to Bill Buckley and moved away in Cordell's direction. Men in the room who had witnessed the savage fight in the street watched him, wondering if the feud was about to be renewed.

Cordell looked up, also, seeing Hamp coming. He sat back in the chair, one hand holding the half-filled liquor glass. Hamp stopped on the other side of the table, looking down at him, and then he said, "Been looking for your man Wynant. He in town, Cordell?"

Lace Cordell stared up at him, hatred in his eyes. "Who said he's my man?" he snapped.

Hamp smiled. "Taking it for granted, Cordell," he said.

"You take a hell of a lot for granted," Cordell told him acidly.

Hamp put both hands on the back of the chair in front of him, and he said slowly, "A man threw a shot at me when I was supposed to be asleep over in the Valley Borax bunkhouse. I took that man to be Wynant. Tell him if he's in Mormon that I intend to shoot him on sight."

"Tell him yourself," Cordell retorted.

"I'll tell him with lead," Hamp said slowly. "I don't know whether you sent him, Cordell, or whether he came on his own, but if you sent him, don't try it again."

The red came into Lace Cordell's bronzed face, and his amber eyes flashed. He put both hands flat on the table, and he said slowly, "Mister, when I want a man dead that badly, I'll kill him myself. I don't like you, Cameron, but I'd never send a man to shoot you in the back. When the time comes I'll be in front of you, and you'd better have a loaded gun."

He was speaking the truth, and Hamp knew it. He had learned what he wanted to know—that Wynant, out of personal hatred, had crept up to the door of the Valley bunkhouse, and then, thinking he'd murdered his man, had not run.

"I'll look for you," Hamp said, "when you come, Cordell."

He left the table and walked out through the doors. Standing on the porch, he saw Stubby McCoy and Steve Beaumont coming up, little Stub already moistening his lips as he neared the saloon.

As they came onto the porch, Hamp steered both of them to the far corner, where they would be alone and out of hearing of other men on the porch.

"What's up?" Stub asked curiously.

"When does the next Imperial wagon leave Mormon?" Hamp asked him. "Do you know their schedule?"

"They got an empty pullin' out at seven," Stub said promptly. "Why?"

"How many water holes they have on their route?" Hamp wanted to know.

Steve Beaumont answered that question. "Only good water," he said, "is at their Yellow Springs station, halfway out to their processing plant. They got another smaller water hole beyond, but it's dry most of the time."

"Imperial depends upon the water in the tank it trails with the rig," Hamp said thoughtfully. "Is that it?"

Beaumont nodded. "Imperial rigs couldn't get fifty miles into the Valley without water tanks. Those tanks carry water out to the stations along the route. Mules can go only so far without water, an' twenty of 'em can drink a hell of a lot."

Hamp nodded. "That's all," he said. He smiled at Stub McCoy and he said, nodding toward the saloon door, "Have one on me, but be ready to ride out of this town at six tomorrow morning."

Little Stub stared at him. "What's up?" he asked again, a light in his blue eyes.

"About time," Hamp told him, "somebody made trouble for Cordell. Be ready to ride."

Stub was grinning, and there was a broad smile on Steve Beaumont's face.

"We'll give 'em hell," Stub chuckled.

"One thing more," Hamp said, his face expressionless.

"Fleming doesn't need to know about this. You boys are riding under my orders tomorrow."

Stub frowned a little, and then he nodded. "Reckon you know what you're doin', Hamp," he said.

They went into the saloon and Hamp stepped off the porch, heading back in the direction of the Valley Borax office. He remained on his side of the street, however, and when he came abreast of the Valley office, he stepped into a darkened doorway.

The lights were still on in the Valley office, indicating that Sheila and Stuart Fleming were still there, and then as he watched the lights went out, and the two of them came out on the walk. Fleming escorted the girl back to the hotel, Hamp watching them from the doorway, and then as Sheila entered the hotel, Fleming crossed the road and stepped into the Piute Saloon, from which Hamp had just come.

Crossing the road, Hamp moved leisurely down toward the hotel, stepped up on the porch, and pulled one of the wicker chairs back into a dark corner. He sat down, touched a match to a cigar, and watched the saloon. From his position he could see in over the bat-wing doors.

Fleming was at the bar, talking with Bill Buckley. After a while Buckley left to make his rounds of the town, and Hamp watched the Sheriff as he moved from saloon to saloon on the opposite side of the street, looking in over the doors, pausing to chat with men on the porch.

A woman was standing out in front of the Twenty Mule Saloon, looking in over the doors, and Hamp saw Bill Buckley stop and talk with her. They both looked into the saloon, and then Buckley put a hand on the woman's shoulder and walked inside.

He came out in a few moments, escorting a strapping fellow in a checked shirt and high boots, a man whom Hamp had seen working in the Valley Borax yard.

Buckley stood with the couple for a few minutes, evidently talking with them, his arm around the big fellow's shoulders, and then the man and the woman went off, the Valley yard man weaving a little.

Hamp Cameron flicked ash from his cigar tip as he watched them go, having read their story. The big fellow from the Valley yard had been drinking up his pay, and his wife had come down to intercede. She had been afraid to enter the saloon, and Bill Buckley had taken a hand, bringing the husband out, talking to him,

157

persuading him to go home with his wife. It had been a nice little insight into Bill Buckley's character.

Buckley went on to the next saloon, stopping to chat with an old man on the porch. Before he went on, he stuck a cigar in the old man's mouth.

Inside the Piute Saloon, Hamp saw Stuart Fleming sit down at one of the card tables, and he realized that the man would be there for some time. The cigar in his mouth, then, he settled himself in the chair, and it was then that he saw Sheila Graham come out of the hotel door and stand on the edge of the porch.

She didn't see him back in the shadows, and she didn't know he was there until he stood up, the wicker chair scraping the floor slightly. He walked toward her, the cigar in his mouth, and he said, "Figured you were in for the night. Put in a pretty long day at the office, didn't you?"

"The room was too hot." Sheila smiled at him. "Thought perhaps I'd take a walk around town before retiring."

Hamp looked across at the Piute Saloon. "South end of town is coolest at night," he observed. "Get a little of the breeze blowing out of Wind Gap." When she didn't say anything, he added, "Could stand a little breeze myself, ma'am."

Sheila Graham nodded. "I do hate to walk around town alone at night," she said.

They left the porch and moved up the walk slowly, and Hamp was thinking as he walked at her side how infrequently he had seen her alone. Almost always, Fleming had been around. He was remembering how gentle and efficient she had been cleaning his wounds after the fight with Cordell. He had to remember, also, that she was engaged to Fleming, and would marry him this winter.

Sheila was saying. "What is going to happen to Valley Borax, Hamp? Can we go on this way?"

"A load came in tonight," Hamp reminded her. "If we can keep the wagons rolling you'll be able to meet expenses and pay off your debts."

"What assurance do we have," Sheila asked, "that the borax will continue to come in? If we lose even one more outfit I'm afraid I'll have to sell out. I've had another offer from a buyer."

"Cordell again?" Hamp asked grimly, and then a drunk lurched out of a nearby saloon, staggering directly toward Sheila. Hamp reached out, grasped the man by the collar, and steered him around the girl. Then ahead of them he saw a man suddenly cross the road in the shadows, and there was something familiar about the man. He was short and slender, and as he moved up a side street, Hamp was almost positive the man had been Merle Wynant, the gun hand.

He was frowning as they walked on again, moving past the few straggling houses at the edge of town. The boardwalk petered out, and then they stopped.

Hamp said, "Far as we go." He turned to face her, expecting that she would immediately begin to retrace her steps back toward the hotel. Instead, she stood where she was, looking up the grade in the direction of Wind Gap and Death Valley. The night air was still hot; even the stars in the sky seemed hot tonight, unlike the

159

cool, cold stars Hamp was accustomed to in the Wyoming skies.

Behind them they could hear the sounds of Mormon, the occasional whoops of laughter, a piano, a man singing. It seemed very far away. To the south lay the desolation of Death Valley, the white stretch of road leading up the grade toward Wind Gap, clumps of mesquite on either side of the road.

They were standing quite close together, much too close together, and even before Hamp Cameron put his hands on Sheila Graham's shoulders, he realized that he should have stepped back.

She looked at him when he turned her around, and he could see the starlight in her eyes, the faint warm breeze ruffling her chestnut hair. He said slowly, "Wish to hell I'd come out here two years ago, before you ever met Fleeting."

Then he bent his head and he kissed her, and for one long moment he thought she would respond to him, and then that moment passed, and he knew that he had been a fool. He said dully, "Reckon I'm sorry, Sheila."

He didn't expect her to, but when they turned around and started back toward the hotel, she took his arm and squeezed it. She said softly, "I was raised in this country, Hamp. I understand its men. It's all right."

They walked on slowly, Hamp staring straight ahead of him, the dull pain again in his heart. He had kissed her, and he had found out. She was still Stuart Fleming's woman.

Chapter Fourteen

At the hotel he said good night to her, and when he turned around he saw Stuart Fleming coming out of the Piute Saloon across the road. Stepping back into the shadows, Hamp watched the Valley superintendent. Fleming had paused outside on the street, looking up and down for a moment, and then he started walking south, the direction from which Hamp had just come with Sheila Graham.

Stepping off the hotel porch, Hamp moved up along the walk on the opposite side of the street. He kept some distance behind Fleming, trying to remain in the shadows as much as possible. When Fleming paused at the first corner to which he came, Hamp immediately stepped into a doorway and waited. He saw Fleming look back as if to make sure that he was not being followed, and then continue on down the street, eventually turning in at the Lucky Dollar Livery.

Crossing the road, Hamp stepped into an alley, moved down it quickly, and when he came out at the other end, turned in the direction of the Lucky Dollar stables. He crossed a vacant lot and then swung around the rear of a long shed that formed one wall of the alley up which Fleming had walked.

There was little doubt in Hamp's mind now that Fleming had arranged to meet someone back here in the Lucky Dollar stables—someone whom he could not afford to meet in public.

Hamp crept toward the corner of the shed. Lantern

161

light from inside the stable flooded a little courtyard here, throwing the shadows of two men outside the open entranceway. One of the men was Stuart Fleming. The other man Hamp could not identify, but he was a big man, as big as Fleming. It was not Lace Cordell, and Hamp experienced a little disappointment, as he had expected Fleming to meet Cordell, thus confirming his opinion that the Valley Borax superintendent was working with the Imperial man.

He could hear the low hum of their voices, but was too far distant to make out what they were saying. Then the man with Fleming left the stable and crossed the courtyard, turning down the alley to the street. Hamp could see him clearly as he crossed the patch of yellow lamplight. The man was Red Doran, the Imperial Borax driver. It meant beyond any shadow of doubt that Fleming was working with Cordell, passing information to him through Doran.

His jaws set tight, Hamp straightened up, and then behind him he heard a tin can being moved slightly by a boot coming toward him. Without turning around, he flung himself away from the shed, rolling on the ground, at the same time sliding the Smith and Wesson from the holster.

A gun roared less than a dozen yards away from where he had been crouching, watching Fleming and Doran. As he rolled on his back he saw the flash of it, bright against the darkness along the wall of the shed.

Another bullet sought him out as he continued to roll on the ground, and then he fired quickly. The killer leaped away from the wall and plunged through the high weeds of the vacant lot beyond.

Scrambling to his feet, gun in hand, Hamp went after him, positive who the man was without even seeing him clearly. The small man leaping with surprising agility through those high weeds, stumbling as he went, was Merle Wynant, and Wynant had taken his last shot at a man from ambush.

As he raced after the little gunman, Hamp saw him stumble and go down among the weeds and rubbish in this vacant lot. Like a cat, then, Wynant whirled and opened fire again. Hamp dropped to the ground, two bullets flying over his head. He fired at the flash of Wynant's gun, and then he squirmed toward the right, his body flat against the ground.

Wynant lay in the deep weeds less than ten yards away, but completely hidden from sight. Very carefully, Hamp inched his way again toward the right, his gun in readiness. He could hear the noise out on the main street, the crowd running toward the alley that led up to this vacant lot, and then he thought of Stuart Fleming, who had been inside the Lucky Dollar stable. Fleming undoubtedly had fled down the alley to the main street when the firing broke out, and was now lost in the crowd.

It would be Hamp's word against Fleming's that the Valley Borax superintendent had met with an Imperial employee, and Sheila Graham could take her pick. Lying there in the high weeds, watching carefully for Wynant's next move, Hamp Cameron thought about that, realizing that he still had nothing definite on Fleming. Fleming could either deny that he had met

Doran or say that he had met him accidentally in the stable, where he had gone to look at a horse.

He was still circling Wynant, moving inch by inch, knowing that the man who sighted the target first and sent the first shot at this distance would come out of it alive. Wynant made no move, so far as Hamp could see. Very possibly the little gunman was waiting for the flash of Hamp's gun so that he could put his own bullets on the target.

Lying flat on his stomach, his head raised very slightly, Hamp peered through the brush, and then he moved again, feeling with his hands before he moved his body so that he wouldn't come in contact with a movable object that would make a noise.

When he stretched out his left hand on one occasion, it came in contact with a smooth, flat stone. His fingers closed around the stone, lifting it, pulling it toward him, and then, holding the Smith and Wesson steady, he tossed the stone a half-dozen feet to his left.

As it struck the ground with a thud, rolling a little, a gun roared from a point ten feet ahead of him. He fired twice at the flash of the gun, and then a man suddenly stood up, stumbled forward, and plunged into the weeds almost at his feet.

He stood up, then, clicking the empty cartridges from the gun cylinder, and he heard Sheriff Bill Buckley's sharp voice from the head of the alley.

"All right," Buckley snapped. "Who's that?"

"Come out," Hamp told him. He was bending down, striking a match, when Buckley came up, and when he held the match close to the face of the man on the ground, he recognized Merle Wynant, his thin face becoming rigid in death.

Buckley said without emotion, "Well, you got him, mister."

"He came up on me from the rear," Hamp explained. "Threw a shot at me."

Buckley straightened up and looked around him. His voice was dry when he spoke. He said, "You takin' a stroll back here in this vacant lot at eleven o'clock at night for any special reason?"

"Followed Stuart Fleming to the Lucky Dollar stable," Hamp told him. "He had a meeting with a man."

"What man?" Buckley asked softly.

"An Imperial driver," Hamp said tersely. "Red Doran."

Sheriff Buckley was silent for a moment as they stood there in the darkness above the dead man. "You hear what they said?" he asked finally.

Hamp shook his head. "Doran left, and then Wynant jumped me. Reckon he's been trailing me for a long time, knowing I was after him."

"He's all through trailin' anyone," Buckley murmured. "An' what do you have on Fleming?"

Hamp was quiet for a moment. Then he said softly, "Getting warm, Sheriff."

Bill Buckley pointed toward the ground. "He was gettin' warm, too, mister," he said quietly. "Be careful."

They left the alley, and Buckley sent the coroner back for the body. A large crowd had gathered on the street, and as Hamp pushed his way through them, he spotted

165

Stuart Fleming. Fleming was looking straight at him.

When he crossed the road to the hotel and went up the steps he saw Sheila Graham standing in the doorway of the hotel. She said when he came up, "I heard the shots. I hope it had nothing to do with our fight with Imperial."

"I killed an Imperial man," Hamp told her simply. "He tried to shoot me down from the rear."

Sheila didn't say anything. She turned and stepped back into the lobby of the hotel, Hamp walking after her. He said quietly, "When a man is paid to kill, he expects to be killed if his luck is bad. Wynant ran out of good cards."

Sheila shook her head. "I—I don't like it, Hamp," she confessed. "Not only that a man has been killed, but that you had to be involved."

Hamp looked at her. "Does it make it any worse that I had to use the gun?" he asked slowly, "rather than McCoy, or Beaumont, or anyone else?"

She didn't look at him, and he noticed that there was a little more color in her face. She said simply, honestly, "It does make a difference, Hamp. I don't want anyone killed, but I hate the thought of you using the gun."

"I don't take any pleasure in it," Hamp murmured, and it gave him a peculiar pleasure that this should affect her the way it did. He could see from the expression on her face that she was really concerned. She did not want to think of him as a killer.

"Will you make me a promise, Hamp?" she said suddenly, and she still wasn't looking at him.

"What is that?" Hamp asked her.

"Will you promise me," Sheila Graham said slowly,

"that you won't use your gun unless you feel that it is absolutely necessary to protect your life?"

Hamp shrugged. "Never use it for any other reason," he stated.

"I don't want you to kill to protect Valley Borax property or interests," Sheila went on. "The company is not worth that much to me."

"When a man is after your money," Hamp observed, "he sometimes has to take your life first. Hard to tell what he's after, and if you wait too long to find out, you're dead."

"I only want you to be careful," Sheila murmured. The door opened behind them then, and they saw Stuart Fleming coming in.

Fleming looked at the two of them, his eyes narrowed, and then he said to Hamp, "You in that shooting, Cameron?"

Hamp nodded. "One of Cordell's gun sharps," he stated. "He's been gunning for me for a long time."

"You follow him back there?" Fleming asked. He was watching Hamp's face closely, trying to learn just how much Hamp had seen from the rear of the shed.

"Wynant followed me." Hamp smiled. He didn't explain what he had been doing at the rear of the buildings along the main street. He let it rest there, leaving the pressure on Fleming. If Fleming wanted to know, he'd have to ask questions, and by asking questions he would point the finger of suspicion at himself.

Fleming said no more on the subject. Turning to Sheila, he said, "Can I have a word with you before you go up, Sheila?

Hamp touched his hat to the girl, and turned and went up the stairs to his room. When he had turned up his lamp he sat down on the edge of the bed, frowning at the far wall. Tonight he had killed his second man in Mormon, and it wasn't going to stop here. Cordell's hired gun hand had been killed; his plans were being upset, and in order to control Death Valley he had to get rid of the only man in his way. There was little doubt in Hamp's mind now that Fleming had sold out to Cordell. The war of attrition would go on, aided and abetted by the Valley superintendent, but first of all they'd have to break the Valley trouble shooter.

Getting up from the bed, Hamp crossed the room and put the back of a chair under the doorknob, and then he hung his gun belt over the bedpost, sliding the gun out of the holster and placing it on the floor within reach of his hand.

He slept soundly, and he was awake a little before dawn, sliding on his boots. He washed at the washstand in the room, and then put on a clean shirt and went downstairs. This was the coolest part of the day, before the sun had come up.

The streets were quite empty as he left the hotel, walked one block north, and then turned down the alley to the Valley Borax yard. He found Steve Beaumont and Stub McCoy in the mess hall, drinking cups of hot black coffee. The cook came in with a platter of bacon and eggs, and Hamp joined them at the table.

Stub McCoy said to him cautiously, "Had a little trouble last night, I hear."

Hamp nodded. "Might have a little more today," he

said. "You ready to ride?"

"Where to?" Steve Beaumont asked him.

"Wind Gap," Hamp told him. "We ride on ahead of that Imperial rig leaving very shortly."

Beaumont moistened his lips. "We gonna raid that rig?" he asked thoughtfully.

Hamp shook his head, a thin smile on his face. "Little target practice," he stated. "Bring rifles with you."

They left the Valley yard twenty minutes later, Hamp with a Winchester rifle in the saddle holster, riding the buckskin again. At seven o'clock in the morning they were moving along the graded road toward Death Valley, with the hot sun just lifting above the rim of the Funerals.

The wind tugged at their hats as they entered Wind Gap. Hamp studied the land on either side. Several hundred yards into the Gap, he turned the buckskin off the road, heading toward a clump of rock on the slope to their left.

They were able to conceal the three mounts behind the high rocks, and then with their rifles crept in among the rocks, taking positions facing the road.

Stub McCoy said softly, "An' here's where we git our target practice, is it?"

"That's right," Hamp said.

"Where in hell is the target?" Stub asked.

Hamp pointed to the dust cloud moving toward them from the direction of Mormon. "Coming up," he said.

In a few minutes the big Imperial rig rolled into sight, two huge empty wagons with the water tank bringing up the rear, the twenty mules hauling the outfit at a fairly fast pace. The driver of the outfit rode up on the seat, with the swamper on the seat of the tandem.

"What happens now?" Steve Beaumont asked. He caressed the barrel of his rifle, and he looked at Hamp worriedly. Then he said reflectively, "Reckon I ain't shootin' a man down from cover, Hamp. I ain't built that way."

"I'll take the first shot," Hamp told him. "You boys hold your fire."

He had the Winchester ready when the rig came down the stretch of road adjacent to their hiding place, a scant hundred yards up the grade. He could see the driver up on the seat, wielding his long whip, cursing at the mules. The swamper, a fat man, was more relaxed on the tandem, his body swaying with the movement of the empty wagon.

Lifting his rifle, Hamp took aim and then squeezed the trigger gently. He sent a second and a third shot immediately after the first, and then grinned as the water suddenly spurted from three holes in the water tank.

Stub McCoy let out a small yelp of satisfaction, and then his Winchester started to crack and more holes appeared in the water tank, the precious water spilling out into the dust of the road.

The rig pulled up suddenly, both driver and swamper hauling on the brakes. Steve Beaumont put two more holes into the water tank, and Hamp said, "Reckon that'll do it."

"Like hell," Stub McCoy muttered. "Look at this, Hamp!"

Hamp Cameron had already seen it. From both supposedly empty wagons men were spilling over the sides, carrying rifles and pistols, darting toward the cover of nearby rocks along the road. Hamp counted eight men coming out of the wagons. With the driver and the swamper, that made a total of ten. They were swarming up the grade, moving from rock to rock, firing as they came, and the bullets were caroming off the rocks around them.

"Little surprise fer us, too," Steve Beaumont murmured. "Reckon we'd better move, Hamp. Lot o' guns down there."

"Let's go," Hamp said briefly.

Turning, they ran back through the rocks to the horses and swung away in the direction of Mormon. Bullets came after them, but the shots were wild, and they were moving fast and were soon out of range.

After they had slowed up a mile or so from the stalled rig, Stub McCoy said, "If they'd o' had ridin' horses in them wagons along with the men hidden there, we'd o' been in a heap o' trouble, Hamp."

Hamp had been riding along silently as they came down onto the road again. He stared straight ahead of him as they moved the horses along at a fast trot. He said then, his voice cold, "Who told Fleming?"

Neither Stub McCoy nor Steve Beaumont spoke, but both of them stared at him. McCoy said finally, "Not me, Hamp."

Steve Beaumont shook his head. "Wasn't me, neither. Didn't tell anybody I was ridin' out—not even the cook this mornin'."

Hamp scowled. "Cordell was expecting trouble this morning," he said grimly, "and he worked the same trick we tried to work on him. How did he know?"

Stub McCoy was frowning. "Didn't tell nobody," he repeated, "exceptin' Miss Sheila. She asked me to come over to the hotel about the time you was havin' this run-in with Wynant. Wanted me to take the train up to Grant City to look at some mules she figured on buyin'. Fleming ain't much of a hand judgin' horseflesh, an' I been helpin' Miss Sheila that way."

"What did you tell her?" Hamp asked slowly.

"Told her you'd planned on goin' into the Valley this mornin', an' maybe givin' one o' the Imperial rigs a little hell."

Steve Beaumont said, "Reckon she could o' spoke to Fleming, Hamp, if you think Fleming is behind it."

"She did speak to Fleming," Hamp told the man tersely. "I left them down in the lobby late last night. She may have mentioned to Fleming that I had something planned for this morning."

"You figure on askin' her?" Beaumont wanted to know. Hamp looked at him. "I'm asking her," he said flatly, "and then I'm speaking with Stuart Fleming."

Chapter Fifteen

They rode into Mormon at ten o'clock in the morning, and as they passed Sheriff Buckley's office, Buckley came out to look at them and lift a hand to Hamp.

Stub McCoy said as they turned down toward the Valley yards, "Reckon we chased that damn Imperial

172

rig back to Mormon, though, Hamp. They wouldn't go into the Valley without water."

Hamp nodded. They had accomplished what he had set out to do, and he experienced some satisfaction from that, but there was a little matter to settle with Stuart Fleming—a matter that had been pending for some time.

In the Valley yard they dismounted, and Hamp walked directly to the office. He found Sheila Graham at her desk, and she smiled at him when he came in. There was no resentment in her eyes over what had happened the previous night. She said, "Good morning, Hamp. I understand you were out early this morning."

Hamp sat on the edge of the desk, his hat in his hand. He said quietly, "Stub McCoy told you last night that we were going into the Valley, possibly to give an Imperial rig a little trouble. Did you tell that to Fleming when you saw him last night?"

Sheila stared at him in surprise. "I believe I mentioned it to him in the lobby after you went upstairs," she said. "What has happened?"

"Cordell had eight men hiding in his empty wagons when we opened fire on his water tank," Hamp told her. "We shot holes into the tank so they couldn't go into the Valley. If we'd been closer that crowd would have shot holes into us. They were waiting for a raid of some kind."

Sheila Graham was looking at him, puzzled. "What has that to do with Stuart?" she asked.

"Fleming was the only one outside of McCoy and Steve Beaumont who knew anything about it," Hamp told her grimly. "McCoy and Beaumont were shot at this morning. Fleming wasn't. Who passed the information on to Cordell?"

"You're joking," Sheila told him simply. "Stuart and I are planning to get married this fall. Why would he work against me and my company?"

"For one reason," Hamp told her, "he knows Valley Borax isn't strong enough to fight Imperial. He wants to merge with Imperial, but he knows you'll never do it. He's either thrown in with Cordell for a big price, or—"

"Or what?" Sheila asked him, face pale, when he hesitated.

"Or he was Cordell's man right from the beginning," Hamp finished, "sent by Cordell to hamstring you after he'd once consolidated himself here."

The thought had come to him quite suddenly, but the moment that he came out with it he was convinced of its truth. Fleming had been with Valley Borax about a year, and now that he had the respect of the men and had won the love of the Valley Borax owner, something he probably hadn't anticipated in the beginning, he could work confidently, knowing that he was beyond suspicion.

"You are making a very serious charge," Sheila said quietly. "I hope, Mr. Cameron, that you are prepared to back it up with proof."

"I saw Fleming speaking with Red Doran, an Imperial driver, last night in the Lucky Dollar stables," Hamp told her. "When we sent the decoy rig out into Death Valley to catch some of the raiders, they knew about it, and until the time that rig left the yard only a few of us were in on the secret—Beaumont, McCoy, Buckley, Fleming, and myself. How did Imperial know enough to let the rig alone?"

Sheila said nothing. She sat behind the desk, her mouth tight, looking straight at him, and he saw the disbelief in her eyes. He realized, then, what a hold Fleming had on her.

"This morning," Hamp went on slowly, "Imperial was expecting a raid on the empty rig going out of Mormon. Only Fleming knew about it, aside from the men who were in on the raid. Does that make sense?"

"Is that all?" Sheila asked him coldly.

"I was set up in Piute City by a bunch of killers," Hamp finished. "The man leading that band was familiar to me. I didn't see him, but I had a glimpse of him in the darkness. He was tall, Fleming's build, and his voice was known to me."

"Stuart's voice?" Sheila wanted to know.

"I couldn't be sure," Hamp told her. "I know that I'd heard the voice before."

"Have you told Sheriff Buckley these facts?" Sheila asked him.

"Most of them," Hamp admitted. "Buckley's been keeping an eye on Fleming, also."

"And does he share your opinion?" Sheila asked rather coldly.

Hamp frowned. "Buckley wants plenty of proof," he admitted.

"How much proof," Sheila Graham said tersely, "should I look for before I condemn the man I am about

175

to marry, who always has had the best interests of Valley Borax at heart?"

Hamp slid off the desk, and he stood there looking down at her. He said quietly, "Figured I'd tell you these things, Sheila, before Valley Borax blew up in your face. A few more raids and you're finished. Is that right?"

"It is true," Sheila admitted.

Hamp put on his hat. "I had to tell you what I thought," he stated, "and what I've seen. Reckon I'm a Valley Borax man, also. I've been shot at because of it. How much lead has Fleming ducked?"

Sheila Graham put out her hand and touched his arm. "I'm sorry, Hamp," she apologized. "It's just that I have a great deal of confidence in Stuart, and this has come rather as a shock. You will admit that even Sheriff Buckley doesn't accept your accusations completely. You've never actually seen Stuart working against Valley Borax, have you?"

"Saw him in Piute City," Hamp told her, "just before this bunch jumped me. Saw him with Doran in the Lucky Dollar stable last night."

The door from the main street opened behind him then, and Fleming came through the door, nodding briefly, coldly, to Hamp. He said to Sheila, "What did you decide about those mules up in Grant City?"

Sheila looked at Hamp, and then at Stuart Fleming. She said quietly, "Stuart, did you meet a man named Red Doran last night in the Lucky Dollar stables?"

Fleming's turquoise eyes flicked. He looked at Hamp before speaking, and then he said casually, "Doran had

176

a riding horse he wanted to sell. I'd arranged to meet him in the stables. Why do you ask?"

Hamp put his hat on, nodded to Sheila, and went out into the yard. He walked over toward the bunkhouse, pausing outside for a drink of water from the big bucket placed there. He was having his second dipperful when he heard someone coming up behind him. Turning his head, he saw Stuart Fleming moving toward him across the yard.

Stub McCoy and Steve Beaumont came out of the bunkhouse, and they looked at Hamp and then at Fleming. Then Beaumont put a shoulder against the doorsill and stood there, watching. Stub McCoy sat down.

Hamp put the dipper back on the hook, and he turned to face Fleming, curiosity running through him. Once before Fleming had made a threat, but Hamp hadn't taken it too seriously then. It was very evident that the Valley superintendent was deliberately walking into trouble now.

He came up, stopping a few feet in front of Hamp, who still stood by the water bucket, and then he said softly, "So you were spying on me."

"Reckon I don't like that word," Hamp told him.

"I don't like a man crawling around behind my back," Fleming said flatly, and he put his cards on the table, leaving it to Hamp to make the next move. Fleming was committed.

"What is it you want, Mr. Fleming?" Hamp asked him.

"How is your face now?" Stuart Fleming wanted to

know. "I believe I made an offer to you some time ago, Mr. Cameron."

Hamp nodded. "Reckon I'm ready to oblige you, Fleming."

Stuart Fleming took off his coat and carefully placed it on the bench next to the dumbfounded Stub McCoy. He put his hat on top of the coat, and then rolled up the sleeves of his shirt.

Hamp took his coat off, also, and put it next to Fleming's. He saw the Valley Borax yard men staring at them, wide-eyed, and then moving toward the scene slowly.

They were like two schoolboys preparing to defend their honor, very punctilious, very grim, very determined. Stuart Fleming stepped away from the bunkhouse and stood watching Hamp. He said softly, "Ready, Cameron?"

"You have yourself a fight," Hamp said, and he moved toward his man. As he did so he saw Sheila Graham come out of the office and stand on the little back porch that opened on the yard. She made no move to come forward or to intervene in this affair. She understood quite clearly that it had to come.

Hamp braced himself, studied Fleming for one moment, sizing him up. They were almost perfectly matched, the same general build, the same height and weight.

The yard men who had gathered to watch said nothing. It was a silent crowd, a crowd of men who liked and respected both of them, and most were stunned by this sight.

Hamp bent in a slight crouch, and then tore in suddenly, driving his right fist toward Fleming's body. He missed, and then he whipped out with his left hand for Fleming's face, and missed with that blow, also, and he did not quite understand that, because he had been on top of his man, and had punched swiftly, savagely.

Fleming's fist snapped against the side of his jaw, and then another fist caught him on the point of the chin, lifting his head toward the sky, and that surprised him too. He noticed that Fleming, as he stepped back, was holding his hands in a peculiar manner, standing straight up, head pulled back, left hand extended, right cocked.

From that posture alone, he realized now that Stuart Fleming knew a good deal about boxing as the professionals boxed. Somewhere back East Fleming had learned how to handle his fists, and for that reason had been very willing to meet Hamp in an engagement like this.

Circling his man, ready to leap in again, Hamp felt some small measure of contempt for him. It was another flaw in Fleming's make-up. He had pushed a fight with another man because he had been confident that his superior talents in the particular craft of boxing would give him the victory. It was no longer a match between two men evenly equipped, but an exhibition of the boxing art by a man who had been trained for such a feat. Fleming again had been underhanded, crafty. He did not ring true.

Hamp tore in at him again, intent on making a fight of it no matter how much ability Fleming had along these lines. He nearly caught Fleming with a hard swinging blow to the head, but Fleming again managed to slide his face away, and as Hamp lunged past he slashed at Hamp's ear with a short, vicious punch.

The earth came up suddenly at Hamp's face, and he rolled as he hit the ground, but he got up immediately and came forward again, though somewhat stunned by the blow.

He realized now that his only salvation lay in getting close to Fleming and hitting away as fast and as hard as he could, but getting close to the man was almost impossible. As he lunged in, Fleming's left fist darted out, catching him in the right eye; it came out again and again, keeping Hamp off, always setting him off balance, and then the right hand whipped up sharply inside Hamp's guard, and his knees buckled.

The yard men watched silently. Hamp was knocked to his knees by a short right to the chin. When he got up, smiling grimly, and tore in with unabated enthusiasm, he ran full into another short, hard right, and the sky exploded in his face. He felt himself falling, and he tried desperately to stay up. The bright, brassy sky overhead was spinning. The nearby yard buildings were moving in a gradually widening circle, and then the blackness closed in on him.

After a while he felt water on his face, and when he opened his eyes he looked up into the wide, homely face of Stub McCoy. Little Stub was wiping his face with a sponge. Steve Beaumont crouched on his heels nearby, a cigarette in his mouth and a frown on his face.

"Comin' around," Stub staid. "Reckon he's all right now," Steve."

Hamp sat up, shaking his head. He noticed that he had been dragged into the shade of the bunkhouse wall. Stuart Fleming was no longer around, and his hat and coat were gone.

"Miss Sheila was over here," Stub McCoy said, "but I told her you were all right."

"Wasn't fair," Beaumont said grimly. "Wasn't fair at all—him fightin' you, Hamp."

Hamp got to his feet, taking the dipper of water Stub McCoy handed to him. He drank it and then felt of his face with his hands. Unlike the fight with Cordell, this fight had scarcely marked him. His left ear felt swollen and his right eye was cut a little, but aside from that he was all right, and there was not that terrible exhaustion which had followed the Cordell fight. He had been beaten by a man who was more clever than he with his fists, but he had not been whipped. He had been rendered unconscious by a clever blow scientifically delivered to a vulnerable spot, but even now he would not acknowledge that Fleming was the better man, and he would fight Fleming tomorrow and the next day, and the day after that, to prove it.

He saw Sheila Graham standing out in front of the office door, looking toward them, and after he had had another dipperful of water he went over to her. He said quietly, "Reckon I kind of pushed that fight, Sheila, and it wasn't good for the company—two of its men fighting each other."

"Are you all right?" Sheila asked anxiously. "I was a little worried before, but Stub told me you'd come around."

Hamp nodded. "Little surprised," he admitted with a grin. "Figured I'd whip him a lot easier than Cordell."

"Then you're not leaving?" Sheila smiled, very much relieved.

"Leaving?" Hamp asked, puzzled. "You want me to go?"

Sheila Graham shook her head. "I was afraid you wouldn't think that you could work in the same company with Fleming after fighting with him."

"Reckon I can stand him," Hamp observed, "if he can stand me."

"I'm glad," Sheila said. "I feel that I really need you here, Hamp. Do—do you still feel the same way about Stuart?"

Hamp looked at her steadily. "I don't change easily," he said. "You know how I feel about Fleming, and about other things."

Sheila looked away, some color coming into her face. "I hope someday," she murmured, "we can straighten things out, Hamp."

He left then, walking up to the main street just in time to see the Imperial rig pulling up in front of Lace Cordell's office. Cordell came out of the office to talk with the driver, and then moved around to the rear to examine the bullet holes in the empty water tank. The men who had been hidden in the two wagons were gone, Hamp noticed, only the driver and the swamper having returned to Mormon.

A small crowd gathered around the rig as Hamp watched from the opposite side of the street. Cordell's face was grim as he spoke with the driver.

Someone came up behind Hamp and said softly, "You reckon that Imperial rig run into trouble out in the Valley, Cameron?"

Hamp turned his head slightly and looked into the cool brown eyes of Sheriff Buckley. "Lost some water," he said.

"Mighty careless, losin' water out in Death Valley," Buckley observed. "An outfit can't go very far without water, now, can it?"

Hamp shook his head.

"You up in Wind Gap this mornin'?" Buckley asked. Hamp nodded. "Shooting at road runners," he murmured.

"Maybe you hit somebody's water tank by mistake," Buckley said. "You remember that, Cameron?"

"Hard to remember." Hamp smiled.

"An' now," Buckley scowled, "you got a borax war on your hands."

Hamp looked at him. "Reckon we've had one for a long time, Sheriff. Now there are two sides fighting."

Bill Buckley shook his head in disgust. "I don't like trouble," he growled. "I like to have peace in my town."

"Valley Borax never asked for trouble," Hamp reminded him, "but now that we're in it, we're in to the finish. Miss Graham wants to keep the company. I aim to see that she does."

"Reckon I want to see her keep it, too," Buckley told him grimly, "but I don't want this town full o' dead men."

Hamp watched him walk away, his homely face worried, and he felt sorry for the man.

Late that afternoon, as he was about to step into the lunchroom, a breed who had ridden in on a sweaty horse handed him a note. It was in pencil, written on a piece of brown paper, and it read, "Come here at once before nightfall. You are in danger."

It was signed, "Rita Sánchez"

Chapter Sixteen

Folding the paper and slipping it into his pocket, Hamp stepped into the restaurant. Sitting down at his corner table, he read the note again. It was in a woman's handwriting, and probably Rita's, but the contents of the note were peculiar. He had nearly been killed in Piute City the last time, and now the Mexican girl was asking him to come out because he was in danger where he was.

It was still another hour or so before nightfall, and he had plenty of time to leave Mormon, but whether he should go was another decision he had to make. It could have been a ruse to get him out to Piute again, but he did not think so. Rita Sánchez had tried to save his life before, and she was doing it again. She had undoubtedly learned through her own sources that he was to be killed that night in Mormon, and hence the urgent request that he come to Piute.

He ate leisurely, and then when he had finished he walked around to the Valley yard, where he located Stub McCoy in the bunkhouse. He had no doubt now that he was being watched in this town, and that leaving it would not be a matter of just saddling a horse and riding

184

out. By doing that he would draw his killers to Piute City.

He said to McCoy, "Saddle my buckskin, Stub, and bring him around to the rear of the Death Valley Saloon a little before dark."

Little Stub stared at him. "What's up?" he asked.

Hamp showed him the note and then tore it up into tiny pieces and tossed the pieces into the fireplace, letting them fall upon dead ashes.

"Rita Sánchez," Stub said thoughtfully. "Reckon I'd do what she says, Hamp. I'll have your horse over there."

Hamp nodded his thanks. He went out, moving back to the main street. The sun was perched on the rim of the Panamint Range to the west. The air was hot and still, so heavy that he felt as if he were wading through it.

The town was coming alive now that the sun was going down. People appeared on the streets. They stood out in front of saloons or on the corners, talking. Horsemen rode in out of Death Valley or from points to the north, their eyes red from the heat, dusty, heading for the saloons.

Hamp saw Bill Buckley out in front of the Piute Saloon, and Buckley smiled and nodded at him as he went by. Passing the Valley Borax office on the opposite side of the street, he saw Stuart Fleming and Sheila Graham inside, and he moved on woodenly, wondering if the day would ever come when Sheila would take his word against Fleming's.

The Death Valley Saloon was nearly empty, although there were quite a few men on the porch outside. At the far end of the bar, drinking alone, he saw the Imperial driver Red Doran, and on an impulse he headed that way.

Doran put his half-empty glass down when he saw Hamp coming up in the bar mirror. He turned slightly to give Hamp a sour glance, and then he put both elbows on the wood, cradling the glass of beer with his big hands.

Stepping up beside him, hooking a finger at a bartender at the other end of the bar, Hamp said casually, "You sell that horse yet, Red?"

Doran looked at him, suspicion coming into his eyes. "What horse?" he asked.

"One you've been trying to sell," Hamp stated. "What's the price?"

Red Doran spat and then said sourly, "Ain't no horse, mister, an' there ain't no price."

The bartender came up and Hamp ordered a beer.

He said to Doran, "Reckon I got the wrong man, Red." When his beer came up, he drank it slowly. Doran's statement meant that Stuart Fleming had deliberately lied to Sheila. His meeting with Doran in the Lucky Dollar stables had had nothing to do with the purchase of a horse Doran owned. On the spur of the moment Fleming had made up that story, just as he would make up other stories to delude Sheila Graham and others into thinking he was a trustworthy Valley Borax man when in reality he was working with Cordell.

Doran left the saloon and Hamp finished his drink. He had a look around the room, and then moved casually toward the other end of the bar, stepped around it, and passed through the door the bartender used to go behind the bar.

A fat bartender with a dirty apron around his waist looked at him in surprise as he entered the storeroom behind the bar. Empty beer barrels, wine kegs, and cases of liquor were piled in this room, and there was a door at one end that apparently opened on the loading platform at the rear of the building. Another door to Hamp's right opened on a corridor leading to other parts of the house.

Lifting a hand to the bartender, who was smoking a cigar back there, Hamp walked toward the first door, opened it, and stepped outside. He saw Stub McCoy just riding up on the buckskin. There was still plenty of light in the sky, but the sun had gone down.

"Obliged," Hamp murmured, and he stepped into the saddle when Stub dismounted.

"Reckon I could ride along," Stub said thoughtfully. "Two guns are allus better than one if you run into trouble."

"Stay in Mormon," Hamp told him. "Watch Fleming. I'll be back after I find out what Rita knows."

"Then what?" Stub asked.

Hamp shrugged. "I'm after a man who will talk about Cordell."

Stub nodded. "Keep yore head down, Hamp," he advised, and then Hamp rode off, moving back into the hills beyond the town with the intention of picking up the old stage road to Piute City later.

When he was a half mile from the town he paused on

a grade to look back, making sure that he was not being followed. He rode on, the darkness closing around him.

Now that he was out of Mormon there was no rush, and he moved along at a leisurely pace, watching the hot stars come out. As he ascended into the hills it became cooler. He rolled a cigarette and put it in his mouth as he rode along, and he considered Rita's message.

Undoubtedly the Mexican girl had learned through one of her informants that an attempt was to be made that night to kill him in Mormon. For that reason she had asked him to come to Piute, where for the moment it would be safer. Whether she knew who was behind the attempted murder or not was another matter.

He figured the time to be nearly ten o'clock at night when he entered Piute, swinging up toward the northernmost street on the side of the notch, a street that was uninhabited as far as he could see.

He dismounted, leading the buckskin by the reins, walking slowly to make no noise, and he walked with his right hand near the gun on his hip.

He heard nothing and he saw nothing, and then he came up behind the sheds to the rear of Manuel's Casino, tying the buckskin in almost the identical spot where he had left the animal on his last visit.

He walked forward then, staying in the shadows along the stables and sheds. A light gleamed in the kitchen window, and he noticed several horses at the hitch racks out front. Looking through the window, he saw Rita talking with fat Manuel, and then Manuel left, going out through the door to the bar.

Hamp tapped on the door gently, and Rita opened it immediately to let him in, relief showing in her eyes when she saw him. She said softly, "You are still alive, Señor Cameron."

"I'm still alive," Hamp smiled. "What was that note about, Rita?"

Rita Sánchez let him into the kitchen, closing the door behind him. She said slowly, "I know only that four men rode in to Mormon this afternoon. They were to kill you in the street tonight."

"Who sent them?" Hamp asked grimly.

Rita shook her head. "That I do not know," she admitted. "I may know in the future."

"I may be dead in the future," Hamp said gloomily. "You sure it wasn't Cordell or even Stuart Fleming?"

Rita looked at him curiously. "I thought Fleming worked for Valley Borax, your company," she said.

"He works for Valley," Hamp scowled, "and he works for himself. I don't trust him."

Both of them, then, heard the horses coming up the street at a hard gallop, swinging around the Casino toward the sheds. Rita Sánchez said tersely, "Go up the stairs."

Hamp raced for the door, out into a corridor, and then went up a short flight of stairs to the second floor of the building. As he leaped up the steps he could hear men breaking into the kitchen below, their boots on the floor. A voice that he recognized distinctly as the voice of Lace Cordell said flatly, "Search the house. See if his horse is out in the sheds."

There were five doors on the second-floor landing.

Hamp opened one of them and stepped into a bedroom that evidently was not in use. The furniture was scattered about the room, several chairs overturned, the room dusty, plaster falling from the ceiling. The light from a hall lamp revealed a sagging bed and a broken table.

Hamp stepped inside, closing the door gently. He crossed the room to the window and tugged at the sash. As he lifted the window gently, he could hear men coming up the stairs at a run.

The window opened on the kitchen shed roof below, and he slipped through, crouching to close it again. Down below he could make out the vague forms of men searching the sheds, looking for his horse, and then he heard Lace Cordell's voice again from the kitchen door:

"Scatter out. He may be hiding."

A man came up and said tersely, "He ain't in the bar."

"He's here," Cordell growled. "We'll tear the house down to find him."

Hamp flattened himself against the wall of the building. He had his gun in his hand now, and he waited, wondering if they would open the window to look out. They couldn't see him from below, as the shadows were very dense at the rear of the house.

He wondered what had brought Cordell after him so quickly, or what had prompted the man to decide that tonight he had to get rid of the Valley Borax trouble shooter. Very possibly the morning raid on the Imperial rig, which Cordell would know had been arranged by Hamp, could have forced him to the decision that the time for raids on stations and stealing mules was over.

Imperial Borax was using guns tonight.

There was also the fact that Red Doran may have gone immediately to Cordell after he had been questioned about the horse, and Cordell, knowing that Hamp had his associate Fleming in a bad spot because of the lie he had told to Sheila Graham, realized that tonight he had to close the books.

They were in the room out of which Hamp had just come. The faint light from the open doorway fell across the shed roof, and he could hear them moving around inside. Now the window was going up.

Gripping the Smith and Wesson in his hand, Hamp flattened his body against the wall and waited. He raised the gun, ready to smash it down across the skull of the man who looked out and saw his boots.

A man did look out, a brief perfunctory glance, and then he pulled his head back in again without seeing Hamp. Hamp lowered the gun. They didn't bother to close the window or the door when they went out.

The gun still in his hand, Hamp lowered himself to a sitting position, put his back against the wall, and relaxed. A man was coming from the direction of the sheds, leading a horse. Hamp recognized the heavy voice of Red Doran.

"He's here," Doran growled. "Found his buckskin tied behind the sheds."

"Girl claims he left right before we came up," Cordell said tersely.

"He ain't goin' far on foot," Doran muttered.

"We'll tear down every house in town to find him," Cordell growled.

A man came from the kitchen, and Hamp heard him say, "He ain't in the Casino, Mr. Cordell. We been all over the house."

"Put a match to it," Cordell snapped. "Burn it down. If he's in hiding, we'll smoke him out."

"What about Manuel?" the man said.

"Let him crawl into another hole in town. I want this place burned down."

Hamp took a deep breath and then crawled slowly out to the edge of the kitchen roof. Lace Cordell was almost directly below him now, less than ten feet away. When Hamp lifted his head slightly he could see the vague shape of the man against the dim light shining from the kitchen.

Another rider was coming up now, dismounting near Cordell, walking toward him, leading his mount. When he spoke, a slow, cold smile came to Hamp's face. The man below who had just ridden up was Stuart Fleming.

Fleming said, "You find him?"

"Not yet," Cordell growled. "We'll catch up with him."

"He can't get back to town," Fleming stated. "If he does, we'll have Buckley on our heels."

Lace Cordell laughed coldly. "If we have to," he snapped, "we'll take care of Buckley, too."

Hamp sat on the roof, listening. Hearing Fleming's voice again at night and in this town, he definitely identified it as the voice he had heard the night the crew chased him through this town. Fleming had tried to kill him that night, just as he was trying to kill him tonight.

Very possibly, Fleming had also been the man who

shot down Piute Charlie from the alley, and Fleming may have thrown that shot at him, Hamp, through the bunkhouse door. Fleming had been very close by that night. And that would account for Merle Wynant's astonishment when Hamp accosted him in the saloon.

All the while it had been Fleming, working for Valley Borax, and undermining it while he made his plans with Lace Cordell. Thinking of that bullet fired through the bunkhouse door, Hamp felt his pulses begin to pound. The cold ruthlessness of the man was revolting. He had made love to Sheila Graham, and he had ruined her financially; he had made promises to her—promises that he probably did not intend to keep. With his smoothness and his false front he had fooled not only Sheila, but even men like Bill Buckley and Stub McCoy and Steve Beaumont.

The protesting Manuel and his few customers were coming out on the porch at the front of the house, Cordell's riders herding them, and then Cordell and Fleming moved away from the kitchen shed, walking toward the front of the building.

"If he's in there," Cordell growled, "we'll burn him out. We'll put a match to the place."

Waiting until they were out of sight, Hamp crawled to the edge of the shed roof, let his body carefully over the edge of the rusted gutter, and then dropped. A portion of the gutter gave way with a wrenching sound as he dropped to the ground, and then a man ran from the shadows near the sheds, calling sharply, "Who's that?

The man was Red Doran. Hamp stood up, gun in hand. He said softly, "You know who it is, Red."

Doran's gun flashed crimson in the dim light, and then Hamp fired also, the boom of his gun mingling with Doran's. The redhead's slug ripped through the dangling gutter above Hamp's head, and then he stumbled forward, clutching at his stomach with both hands, dropping his gun, muttering something to himself.

Hamp raced toward the sheds, hoping to pick up a horse there and make his getaway. Two men suddenly appeared from the corner of one of the sheds, and he had to veer off away from them, running back toward the opposite corner of the Casino.

A man yelled, "That's him!"

A bullet followed, but Hamp was already around the building, racing up the street. He could hear men calling behind him as he ran, turning into an alley and ascending the grade to the next street on the side of the notch.

As he turned into this street he spotted a large, rectangular building on the right, a two-story structure. It had undoubtedly been some kind of auditorium, and he ran toward it, going up the rickety wooden steps and past the big doors, one of which was hanging on one hinge.

There was a ticket booth just inside the door with a caged window looking toward the entranceway. Hamp stepped into the booth, drawing the Smith and Wesson, and he stood behind the little window, the muzzle of the gun pointing through the opening.

The faint light from a crescent moon illuminated the entranceway, but Hamp, standing inside the booth, was completely hidden from sight. He waited, hearing men running past the building. On one wall, where the light came in, he could see a torn, faded poster on which were printed the words "Opal Opera House."

The voices died away outside as Cordell's men moved up the street, but he waited inside the booth, knowing that they would come back, checking through each building when they couldn't find him. His strategy now lay in hitting them one at a time, staying alive as long as he could, and hoping Bill Buckley would be in the vicinity and come into the fight.

At the other end of the street a jittery gunman started to throw lead at a shadow, but he stopped when someone cursed him out. And then again he heard Stuart Fleming's voice outside the opera house, and the anger surged through him. He had promised Sheila Graham that he would be very careful, and that he would not kill a man unless that man was attempting to kill him. Stuart Fleming was tracking him down tonight with a gun in his hand.

There were steps on the walk outside, coming up the stairs toward the ticket booth. Hamp saw the shadow and then the man coming in slowly, passing through a patch of light. The man was Stuart Fleming. A gun gleamed in his hand.

Fleming walked past the ticket booth, pausing within eighteen inches of Hamp, and then moving down past the scattered, overturned chairs in the auditorium.

Hamp turned gently, facing the little door through which he had come. He could hear Fleming's footsteps moving across the floor, and then the footsteps stopped.

They started up again as Fleming retraced his path, coming back to the entranceway. Again Hamp turned carefully inside the booth, sliding the gun barrel through the ticket slot.

Fleming passed the booth, walking slowly, listening, his gun still in his hand, and as he walked toward the door, Hamp called after him softly:

"Forgot your ticket, Fleming."

Fleming swung around, firing wildly, not even seeing Hamp. One bullet ripped through the wire cage over Hamp's head. Another gouged wood from the wooden framework of the cage, and then Hamp fired twice, carefully, steadily, at a distance of six feet.

Fleming staggered and then lurched toward the booth, Hamp still covering him with the Smith and Wesson. Fleming put one hand on the cage window, gripping the bars with his fingers, and he strove desperately to lift the gun in his other hand up to the ticket slot.

He couldn't do it, though, and as he started to sag toward the floor, Hamp, said to him softly, "There's your ticket, Fleming—to hell."

When Fleming's body hit the wooden floor with a thud, Hamp slipped out the back door of the little booth and ran down through the auditorium, going up a flight of small steps to the stage and then around a moth-eaten curtain to the rear of the stage.

At the other end of the building he could hear men coming in, their boots resounding hollowly on the wood floor. There was a pause when they found Fleming's body, and then they came on again, more slowly now, trying to ferret him out in the darkness. He could hear them stumbling over chairs, cursing, and then Lace Cordell's flat, heavy voice said, "Two of you

196

get up those stairs to the right."

Stepping in through the open door of one of the dressing rooms, Hamp located a window. There were several closets in the room, used to store costumes, and he opened one of them, feeling around inside.

Then, picking up a chair, he smashed out the window, tossed the chair through, and then stepped quickly over to the closet, entered it, and closed the door.

The sound of shattering glass drew Cordell's men toward the room. They came running, and Hamp heard one of them yell, "He went out through that window!"

Several men entered the room to look out the window, but the others were already running back toward the main entranceway so that they could cut around to the rear.

Waiting until the last man had left the room, Hamp opened the closet door and stepped out. Moving back to the main auditorium, he located a stairway leading to the balcony, and he ascended the stairway, fumbling around in the darkened balcony until he found a seat. In the darkness, then, concealed from the floor below, he rolled a cigarette, touched a match to it, and blew the match out immediately. He was still alive.

Chapter Seventeen

Finishing the cigarette five minutes later, Hamp rubbed it out on the floor of the balcony and stood up. Cordell and his crew were still in the vicinity, but he hoped they had split up again in their search for him. His only hope for survival tonight lay in dividing the force against him, and then hitting at them singly.

Moving down the rickety stairs from the balcony to the main floor, he picked his way carefully through the scattered, broken chairs to the main entrance. Stuart Fleming still lay where he had fallen, on his face, arms outstretched, and looking at him, Hamp wondered how Sheila Graham was going to take this. He had killed Fleming, but Fleming had sought to kill him, coldly, deliberately, tracking him down with Lace Cordell's hired gun hands. He hoped that Sheila would understand this.

Looking out through the open doorway, he noticed that the street was empty. Cordell's crew must have moved to the far end of the street, or possibly they had even ascended the grade to the next street in their search for him. He was positive, though, that they had not given up, and that they had rounded up every horse in the vicinity, making sure that he could not steal one and return to Mormon.

Stepping out of the opera house, Hamp moved into the shadows along the wall of the nearest building, walked to the end of the street, and then crossed over quickly. As he did so he heard a man calling from the street above, the highest of the three streets in Piute City, and he knew that Cordell's crew was up there.

Returning to the main street, he made his way back to Manuel's Casino, and as he drew near, moving along the north side of the street, he saw Rita Sánchez standing on the porch, her tall body tense, and he realized that she was listening for the shots—shots that would tell her that he, Hamp Cameron, was dead.

Pausing at the far end of the porch, and still in the shadows, he called softly, "Rita."

She didn't move at first, and he thought she hadn't heard him, and then she moved in his direction, still up on the porch, and she stopped a few feet from where he was crouching at the base of the porch. She said softly, without looking in his direction, "Señor Cameron. I am glad you are still alive."

"They watching the horses in the back?" Hamp asked her.

"Two men," Rita told him. "Do not try to leave on foot. They will run you down before morning after they've searched every house in town."

"Didn't figure on walking back to Mormon," Hamp said dryly. He scratched his chin thoughtfully, and then he added, "Reckon I'll have a look at those two boys in the back."

"There were six of them went after you," Rita told him, "when you escaped from here."

"Five now," Hamp murmured, and then he heard the horsemen hammering in from the far end of town. "Better get back inside," he said to Rita. "We'll see who this is."

Rita left him, walking back toward the bat-wing doors. She didn't go inside, and Hamp watched her for a moment before turning his attention to the riders coming up. He wondered if one of them would be Bill Buckley coming in to Piute.

They were moving fast, and as they came into the light from the Casino front he recognized them as Steve Beaumont and Stub McCoy. Both men dismounted in front of the hitch rack, and as they did so, one of the guards that Cordell had stationed at the sheds in the rear came running around the corner.

Stepping out on the walk, gun in hand, Hamp yelled, "Watch it, Beaumont!"

The Valley yard man had ducked under the rack and was coming up on the walk when he heard Hamp's voice. Dropping to his knees, he drew his gun just as the guard fired at him.

Hamp fired twice, and the guard dropped to his knees, the gun sagging in his hand. The second guard broke around the corner just as the first man fell to the walk. Steve Beaumont had his gun on this man, holding his fire until the man threw a quick, wild shot in his direction, and then he fired calmly from a squatting position, his first shot doubling up the gun hand, sending him staggering back into the shadows.

Hamp came down the walk, shoving fresh cartridges into his gun. He called to Rita Sánchez, who was still outside the door, "Better get inside, señorita."

Stub McCoy came up on the walk, gun in hand. The little man said casually, "What in hell's goin' on here, Hamp? We heard them guns bangin' 'way down the stage road an' we come runnin'."

"Cordell's crew is here hunting me down," Hamp told him. "Reckon they'll be along here in a minute or two."

Steve Beaumont said grimly, "So they're out in the open, are they, Hamp?"

Hamp nodded. "Fleming was with them," he stated. He snapped the Smith and Wesson shut and slid the gun back into the holster.

"He *was* with 'em?" Stub McCoy asked slowly.

"He's dead," Hamp said quietly. "It's only Cordell and four or five of his gun hands coming up on us now."

Steve Beaumont stared up the dark street. From the north end of town they could hear men calling to each other.

Beaumont said without emotion, "So Fleming was Cordell's man."

Hamp nodded. "Right from the beginning, I'd say. He's been after my hide for a long time. I believe he was the one tried to put a bullet through me when I was asleep in the bunkhouse. He was hunting me down in this town once before."

"That's how come Cordell's bunch knew all the time what was goin' on with us." Beaumont scowled. "He was workin' against the girl he was supposed to be marryin'."

"Why?" Stub McCoy asked bluntly.

Hamp shrugged. "A man will do 'most anything for a million dollars," he observed. "If Cordell and Fleming controlled the borax of Death Valley, they'd make that much and more. Maybe he figured he could play both ends against the middle and still win out. He figured wrong."

"How many comin' this way?" Beaumont asked. "An' how do we take 'em, Hamp?"

"Count on five," Hamp told him. "Too many for you?"

"Hell." Beaumont smiled. "Wasn't for you, was it?"

Hamp said to Stub McCoy, "Take those horses around to the back, Stub, and then wait in the alley across the road. You can get into one of the buildings on this side of the street, Steve."

"What about you?" Beaumont wanted to know.

"I'll be inside," Hamp told him. "If the bunch of them come up on the porch, you can give them some lead. If Cordell enters the Casino alone, let him go."

Steve Beaumont and McCoy looked at each other, and then Stub shrugged. He walked around toward the sheds with the two horses, and Beaumont moved down the walk, entering a vacant building.

Hamp went up the steps, pushing through the batwing doors of the Casino. Rita Sánchez was standing just inside. Manuel was behind his bar, his black, smoky eyes expressionless.

Hamp said to the girl, "Better get in the kitchen and take your uncle with you."

"They are coming here?" Rita asked.

Hamp nodded.

Rita looked at him curiously. "You are ready to die for this woman?" she asked.

Hamp shrugged. "You work for an outfit," he said, "and that's your brand. You stay with it."

Rita laughed a little. "It is fortunate, however," she said, "that your brand includes a girl like Miss Sheila Graham. Is it not, Señor Cameron?"

Hamp didn't say anything, but as he walked around the bar, motioning for Manuel to step into the kitchen, he was considering the fact that with Fleming out of the way, he did have a clear path ahead of him.

Rita and her uncle stepped into the kitchen, closing the door behind them. Hamp took off his hat and placed it on the bar; he slipped the Smith and Wesson from the holster and placed it next to the hat, and then he took a bottle from the shelf behind him, opened it, and poured himself a drink. He didn't drink the liquor, however.

Leaning on the bar, arms crossed in front of him, he faced the door. His hands were a matter of inches from the gun in front of him. He stood there, motionless now, giving Lace Cordell the break Cordell would never give to him tonight.

He heard them coming up, moving slowly now because they weren't sure what they were running into. From the upper part of town they had heard shots, and they could not be sure who had done the shooting. They would be cautious.

Hamp waited. He heard boots on the steps, and then low voices, and he braced himself behind the bar, wondering if he would ever get to drink that liquor in front of him; wondering, too, if he would ever get to see Sheila Graham and explain what had happened to Fleming.

A man was coming across the porch toward the batwing doors, his footsteps resounding hollowly on the wood, and then the top of his hat and his face appeared over the doors.

The man was Lace Cordell, his wide, bronzed face sweaty from his exertions this night, his amber eyes hard. For one brief moment as he pushed in through the doors he didn't particularly notice Hamp behind the bar, or seeing him, did not connect him with his present mission.

Then he stopped, and one of the doors swinging back

struck him lightly. He stared at Hamp behind the bar, his eyes flicking to the gun on the bar, and then a slight grin almost of appreciation came to his face. His right hand moved for his gun, and moved very fast—faster than Hamp had anticipated. Lace Cordell threw the first bullet.

The mirror behind Hamp shattered as the slug missed his head by inches. He fired at Cordell from a distance of thirty feet, his hand resting on the bar, the gun steady, and he needed but one shot.

Cordell's gun hand dropped, the muzzle of the gun pointing toward the floor. He frowned at Hamp and then reached up with his free hand to grasp the top of the batwing door to his left. He took one step backward, his mouth beginning to work, and when he fell he tore the door from the hinge and he lay there with it across his chest, the gun still in his right hand.

Outside, guns began to bang. A man yelled, "We're in a pocket!"

Stub McCoy was firing from the alley across the road, and Beaumont had opened up from the vacant house. Hamp vaulted the bar and sprinted toward the door, gun in hand.

Outside on the walk he saw five men, one of them already down and another man clutching his right shoulder where he had been hit, writhing in pain. A man sat on a horse out in the middle of the road, a six-gun smoking in his hand, and when the horse came out into the light, Hamp recognized the man as Bill Buckley.

The Sheriff of Mormon was saying crisply, "Throw them guns down, boys."

When Hamp came out through the door, stepping past the body of Cordell, the three gun hands remaining let their guns fall to the boardwalk. Stub McCoy and Steve Beaumont came up as Buckley was dismounting at the hitch rack, and little Stub picked up the guns.

Bill Buckley said grimly, "Hell of a lot o' shootin' around this way, Cameron. Been tryin' to find out who's shootin' at who."

"All over now," Hamp told him.

Buckley looked at the body of Lace Cordell, and then he said dryly, "Figured that. Maybe it's good I came up a little late. Saw everybody leavin' town, headin' fer Piute, an' I came along."

"We follered Fleming out here," Stub McCoy volunteered. "You told me to keep an eye on him, Hamp."

Buckley looked at Hamp. "What about Fleming?" he asked.

"Dead," he said. "He was Cordell's man."

Bill Buckley nodded. "Reckon you had it right from the beginning, Cameron. We'll get these boys back to Mormon, an' they'll talk some more fer us."

Hamp saw Rita Sánchez coming out on the porch now, and he lingered behind as Buckley, Beaumont, and Stub McCoy tied the three Cordell men to their mounts and pointed them toward Mormon.

Rita came out with the glass of liquor he had left on the bar. She had a glass for herself, and she held up the glass and said to him, "To your lady."

"And to you," Hamp told her, "another lady. I am obliged for your help, señorita."

Rita inclined her fine head slightly. "I wish you much happiness," she said.

Hamp rode on, then, catching up with Buckley and the Valley men. They entered Mormon late at night and Hamp went immediately to the hotel, knowing that he had to break the news to Sheila.

When he knocked on her door, she answered it at once, and he realized that she had been awake, waiting for news from Piute City. She wore a nightgown and her chestnut hair was tied in pigtails, making her look very young.

Hamp closed the door behind him, and he stood there, his hat in his hand. He said slowly, "I don't bring you good news, Miss Graham."

Sheila Graham looked at him steadily, and then she sat down on the edge of a chair. She said, "All right."

Hamp told her the story of the fight in Piute City, and of his first sight of Fleming with Lace Cordell as they sought to kill him at the Casino. When he told her of the shooting in the opera house he noticed that her shoulders drooped a little and she grew more pale. She didn't say a word until Hamp had finished. Then she stood up again, and she said slowly:

"I'm afraid I have wronged you, Hamp, and I'm sorry. You've been the one who has worked for Valley Borax all the time."

"My outfit," Hamp told her. He put his hand on the doorknob, and then he paused. He said, "Anything I can do . . . I know how you feel tonight, Sheila."

"It's not as bad," Sheila told him quietly, "as you might have imagined, Hamp. It is, of course, a shock, but I believe you rather prepared me for it before when you accused Stuart of working with Cordell. I've been thinking about that a great deal since you spoke to me."

"He wanted the big money," Hamp said, almost as if he were apologizing for the man.

"I know." Sheila nodded. "I knew him, Hamp, not as well as I should have, but I did know him."

She stood there with the lamplight on her hair, tall and still, and Hamp Cameron knew that someday he would speak to her. Not now, of course, but someday when the horror of this night was erased from her mind, when peace reigned in Death Valley, and the Valley Borax wagons were running on schedule—his schedule. He would tell her, then, what was on his mind tonight, that he thought she was the most beautiful and the most desirable woman in the world.

"If you need me," Hamp Cameron said, "I'll be around."

"I know," Sheila murmured, "and I'm grateful, Hamp. I'm grateful for everything."

When he looked into her eyes, he knew that when the time came for him to speak he would find her receptive. He knew that as certainly as he knew that the graded road in and out of the valley of hell was open and safe.

Center Point Publishing
600 Brooks Road ● PO Box 1
Thorndike ME 04986-0001 USA

(207) 568-3717

US & Canada:
1 800 929-9108